"Some very dangerous people know about the chocolate diamond. If I hadn't reached you first, it would be even worse, trust me. And you do need to trust me, do you understand?"

Trust him? Cullen had come in here demanding a hunk of a diamond that she figured didn't even exist and now he had thugs looking for him and this alleged diamond and he wanted her to trust him? Right.

She stared up at him. She could imagine him doing bad things, very bad things. He had that kind of look about him. Half treasure hunter, half pirate. All male.

"I won't go anywhere with you," she said, wondering about the lesser of two evils.

He sighed. "I don't have time to argue with you. If you don't do as I say, they will either torture you or kill you. Or both."

The banging ended and the sound of crashing glass took its place.

"What's it going to be, Esther?"

Books by Lenora Worth

LENORA WORTH

has written more than forty books for three different publishers. Her career with Love Inspired Books spans close to fifteen years. In February 2011 her Love Inspired Suspense novel *Body of Evidence* made the *New York Times* bestseller list. Her very first Love Inspired title, *The Wedding Quilt,* won *Affaire de Coeur*'s Best Inspirational for 1997, and *Logan's Child* won an *RT Book Reviews* Best Love Inspired for 1998. With millions of books in print, Lenora continues to write for the Love Inspired and Love Inspired Suspense lines. For years Lenora also wrote a weekly opinion column for the local paper and worked freelance with a local magazine. She has now turned to full-time fiction writing and enjoying adventures with her retired husband, Don. Married for thirty-six years, they have two grown children. Lenora enjoys writing, reading and shopping... especially shoe shopping.

LENORA WORTH

THE DIAMOND SECRET

Love Inspired

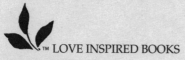

™ LOVE INSPIRED BOOKS

Recycling programs for this product may not exist in your area.

ISBN-13: 978-0-373-44500-4

THE DIAMOND SECRET

www.LoveInspiredBooks.com

Printed in U.S.A.

I will give you treasures that are hidden away
in dark places. I will give you riches
that are stored up in secret places.
—*Isaiah* 45:3

To my editor, Patience Bloom. Thanks for encouraging me, believing in me and letting me have fun with words. You are a true precious jewel!

ONE

Somewhere in the Quarter, a lonely saxophone wailed a bluesy tune.

Esther Carlisle listened to the sweet notes hitting the late-afternoon wind, then glanced at the pendulum clock ticking away the seconds behind the counter. Soon all of the clocks would start chiming the top of the hour.

Time to close up shop and go home. Or maybe, go upstairs to the apartment she'd inherited along with this shop after her father had died last year. She'd managed to avoid the apartment for months. But Carlisle Collectibles had become her life lately. Royal Street had always been her street anyway since she'd grown up hanging out here in this big, rambling shop. She knew the shopkeepers, and even the homeless people, by name. And she could set her own antique pendant watch by that saxophone player's daily schedule. Harold was a war veteran. He slept until the sun started settling behind the buildings then got up to fill the night with notes. His soulful melody merged with the sound of voices carrying out on the street and the honking of horns up on Canal.

He'd probably never understand why Esther prayed for him on a daily basis. But he did seem to understand that she was aware of him, since she often placed dollar bills in his open saxophone case. Her devout father had taught her the golden rule, after all. In return, because Esther tried to be kind to all she met, the rough, quirky crowd in the Quarter watched over her.

"Another quiet summer day in the French Quarter," she said, the echo of her statement hitting the high rafters and the tall windows to reflect back on her while the clocks kept on tick, tick, ticking all around her.

The pendulums would always swing back. Tomorrow, she'd have some time off to work in her big studio in the Garden District, to create art out of broken pieces of life. One of her sculptures was on display in the front window of the shop. The whimsical piece she called *Wasted Time* was made from old watches, ancient keys and intricate antique glass doorknobs of various shapes and sizes. It represented missed opportunities and time passing without change.

It also represented her mood these days.

The phone rang, jarring her back to the here and now.

"Esther, how was your day?"

Mr. Reynolds, from next door. He always called to check on her. Especially when he knew her assistant, Ted, wasn't in.

"I'm good. A slow day here. How about you?"

"A few takers," the distinguished history buff replied. "Sold a few soldiers. Had a few lookers—one in particular. Bought a nice 1858 Remington revolver."

"Wow, that's a true gun buff, Mr. Reynolds."

They had a friendly competition going since they both carried antique weaponry.

"Yes. He was a very interesting man. Surprised he didn't come down your way."

"Nope. I'm about to close."

Esther hung up, then finished tallying the receipts of the day, worried because she'd had so few visitors. But things would pick up later in the season. Right now, she only wanted to lock up and head home for some dinner and a cup of tea. Maybe she'd read that book she'd found at the bookstore down the way. Or maybe go into the tiny courtyard studio she'd set up out back and work on one of her less complicated pieces. She could go to the potluck supper held in the tiny chapel near her home in the Garden District. Or she could tackle all the papers and unopened mail that had been piling up on her father's rolltop desk.

Humming "Unforgettable" along with the saxophone, Esther walked up the planked aisle, her footsteps marking time along with the clocks, and pushed at the rickety old glass paneled door.

A hand shoved at the outside knob.

She glanced up to see the silhouette of a tall man wearing a snazzy fedora. A chunky cover of dark bangs hid his eyes, but she didn't miss the flash of a smile and the gleam of white teeth. "Wait, may I come in?"

Esther stopped, stared, shook her head. "Sorry, I'm closing for the day." She glanced at her watch. "It's five o'clock."

The man stood back to read the sign on the door. "You *close* at five. It's five till."

Letting out a long-suffering sigh, Esther stepped back. "Give me a break, will you? I'm tired. I'll be back tomorrow at nine, I promise."

He put his arms across his chest, his biceps bulging with authority against his black T-shirt. "Give *me* a break. I've traveled a long way to get here."

Okay, he had an intriguing accent. Irish maybe? And he did have that whole Indiana Jones thing down pretty good. The fedora was classic and classy and old and worn enough to be endearing. The black T-shirt looked to be made of silk. And the slightly worn khaki cargo pants could have stepped right out of a J. Peterman catalogue. As well as the buttery leather travel satchel swung over his shoulder. His broad, nice-looking shoulder. Which was underneath his interesting, scarred face and ink-washed black hair and those oh-so-gray-blue eyes that seemed to zoom in on Esther. And how could she miss the self-assured grin he wore with all the finesse of a pirate.

An adventurer? A pirate? Or someone pretending to be something he could never be? Like her dear, departed father.

"We're closed," she said again. But she didn't try to shut the door in his face. His bronzed, sun-crinkled, mighty fine-looking face. Was she so pathetic that she'd fall for that face and let him in so he could spend an hour of her precious time walking the aisles in search of something old that he wouldn't buy anyway?

"I need to ask you a few questions, Miss Carlisle."

Shocked, she stood her ground. "You know my name. Why don't I know yours?"

He shot her a swagger of a grin. "Probably because I haven't properly introduced myself. Cullen Murphy." He glanced up and down the busy street, intensity misting around him like humidity. "May I please come in? I'll only be a minute or two."

"Uh-huh." She'd heard that before. Collectors, by nature, could never spend a minute or two in an antiques shop. Carlisle Collectibles had a good reputation for carrying the finest antiques, estate jewelry and trinkets, so anyone coming here would want to explore until their heart's content.

But she wasn't sure yet about this one. Did he have a heart underneath all that manly ruggedness? Or had she read one too many romance novels?

He didn't move to leave.

She didn't move to let him in.

"This is really important," he finally said, edginess cutting through his voice. "I can't come back tomorrow."

"What exactly are you looking for?"

"Who said I was looking for anything?"

"You surely didn't come here to chat with me, right?"

"Uh, no. Not that that wouldn't be pleasant. I'd like to talk to you, but I'm kind of in a rush."

She waited.

"Okay, I need to see your vintage diamond collection."

That surprised her. "Which one? We have several."

"Persia. Circa 1500 B.C."

Something akin to a warning tickled her spine. Esther stepped back a pace and the door creaked open before she could stop it. "That is way vintage. You must be joking." She hoped so. She didn't like where her thoughts were taking her.

He was inside before she even blinked. "I can assure you, I'm not." He immediately started looking over her, around her and through her. "I'll only take a moment."

"Yeah, I got that." With a sigh and a bit of curiosity, she allowed him to stay. But she locked the door and put out the Closed sign anyway.

Cullen Murphy scanned the big, tastefully cluttered shop that was reputed to be one of the premiere antiques stores in New Orleans, maybe in the South, according to everything he'd heard from Jefferson Carlisle. But Cullen didn't care about dainty teacups or two-hundred-year-old sideboards. He only had one prize in mind. This woman's father had hidden that prize and Cullen had to find it before anyone else did. And since he had some very nasty people hot on his trail, now would be a good time.

If he could get past Lady Golden Eyes. She obviously had no clue why he was here. That was good, for her sake, at least. Giving her another covert glance, he noted that behind those granny glasses, she did indeed have golden eyes. And a cute little tulip of a face. Her long hair, tucked back from her face in an oh-so-proper coil at the nape of her kissable neck, sparkled with all the color of rich, shining copper while the scent of jasmine and spice sizzled all around her in an intoxicating cloud.

Why did he have to stop and smell the perfume?

No time for that kind of entertainment, however. He'd prepared himself for getting to know Esther Carlisle, but now he reminded himself he didn't like emotional entanglements. So…on to the job.

He needed to find that diamond.

"If you could tell me why you're here, Mr. Murphy…" she said from behind him, that exotic scent making him think of faraway places.

He turned, brusque and to the point. "Cullen, please. I'm an archaeologist and I also enjoy collecting rare jewelry, specifically diamonds." Thankfully, these days he collected exotic gems the old-fashioned way—legally.

"You did mention diamonds," she said, hurrying to the long jewelry counter, her every move as tightly coiled as the annoying, whining clocks lining the walls and shelves. "I'll show you what I have and then, I'm closing. Deal?"

"Deal," he said, holding out his hand.

She took it, stared at it as if it were a snake and then shook it, her tiny grip surprisingly strong. "You said you'd come a long way?"

"Aye. All the way from Dublin, luv."

Her catlike eyes widened at that. "Dublin, Ireland. Well, we have a couple of exquisite pieces reputed to be from Persia, very old and amazingly huge, but I don't think we have anything dating back thirty-five hundred years. Most pieces such as that belong in a museum. Exactly what kind of diamond are you looking for?"

Cullen whirled and took off his hat, then dropped his satchel on the counter. "A chocolate one."

Chocolate?

He did mean business. But surely he couldn't be searching for the one diamond Esther had put out of her mind long ago. Chocolate diamonds, a rich sparkling golden-brown in color, were very rare indeed. Rare and beautiful. Her father had been fascinated with a certain rare chocolate diamond.

Esther pointed to her diamond collection on display in a glass-sealed, secure case. "I don't know if I have any chocolates. They're extremely hard to come by."

While her handsome guest studied the sparkling jewels inside the locked cabinet, she studied him. He was all alpha male, stalking the jewels like a big cat. He seemed to fill the huge vastness of her shop, making everything shrink.

Especially her.

Esther felt tiny and invisible with such raw power crashing into her staid, boring world. The sound of the ticking clocks seemed to vanish into the dusty recesses of the building, only to be replaced with the drum, drum, drumming of his fingers against the double-paned glass. Was she having an incredible dream or was this man really flesh and blood? And could his purpose for being here center on a crazy folktale?

The very folktale that ultimately destroyed her father?

Confused but calm, she blinked and tried to assert her authority. "Can you describe this particular diamond?"

He stared into the lit showcase, the glow from the spotlights causing his dark face to look almost sardonic. Almost.

"It's close to fifty carats, loose, not set. Rectangular in shape. Possibly a ragged-type rectangle." He stood to turn toward her. "Have you ever heard of the chocolate diamond that was supposedly a part of the treasure the pirate Lafitte hid somewhere on Barataria Bay?"

Esther's hand went to her mouth. "Oh, *that* diamond." Her worst assumptions had been confirmed. She grew warm. Her pulse beat a rapid path against her temples.

Her father had been obsessed with the stories of the ancient fifty-carat diamond. But he'd never been able to find it. Mainly because he'd never actually searched for it. He'd mostly enjoyed speculating about the myth and the legend of such a jewel, to the point of becoming completely obsessed. And quite ill before he'd died. How could she have forgotten all of his late-night stories and conspiracy theories?

Maybe because she'd blocked a lot of unpleasant memories? She'd certainly tried to put that particular bedtime story away for good. And that was the main reason she'd stayed away from his office upstairs.

"That'd be the one," Cullen replied, intensity oozing out every pore. He studied her as if expecting her to jump up and down in delight. "I've done a lot of research and traced it back to Louisiana. Do you know of it?"

Esther almost giggled, but it was nervous laughter not happiness. "Everyone around here knows of it. But that's a legend, part of the folklore that swirls around Lafitte."

"I believe it exists," Cullen said, his tone serious.

"I can see that," Esther retorted, tired of this foolishness and determined not to get sucked into the absurd story again. "It might exist, but I can assure you I don't have it here." If her father had ever gotten up the gumption to search for the elusive diamond and if he'd found it, she would have known.

"I was told—"

Her heart did a little spin of a warning. "Whoever sent you here was mistaken."

"Are you sure about that? I mean, this is a very important diamond, a true piece of history."

"I understand that, but I don't have it. I've read about it, mostly from books and research my father gathered. He enjoyed musing about the diamond. It's reputed to have possibly been one of the jewels on the garment of one of the high priest from the Twelve Tribes of Israel—the Levi tribe, I believe. In fact, my father called it the Levi-Lafitte Diamond."

His eyes widened in appreciation. "You do know your stuff. While that has never been substantiated, there *was* a diamond on the second row of each of the breastplates. This particular chocolate could have been light in color, but still it's what we now call a chocolate diamond."

"Thanks," she said with a tad more sarcasm than she'd intended. Of course, she knew her stuff. Her father had breathed these types of ridiculous tales and he'd often told them to her, always stressing that she shouldn't repeat his theories. Her father, rest his sweet soul, had always been a speculative dreamer.

And so was the treasure seeker standing beside her. He leaned close, his eyes going velvety dark. "It's rumored that Lafitte discovered that very diamond in his travels. Maybe stole it from a king or some exotic Persian prince. That's the last place it was supposedly seen, hence the circa 1500 B.C."

"And you think I have it because…?"

Cullen turned to stare at her, his fingers still tapping on the glass counter. "Because I knew your father. He was a brilliant historian and also a collector. I corresponded with him a lot before he died. He enjoyed discussing the possibilities of the diamond's existence." He paused. "I was sorry to hear of his heart attack."

Touched, but shocked that this man had known her father and hadn't told her that right away, Esther looked toward the back of the cavernous building. "Thank you. He got so sick, but he wouldn't go to the doctor. He died here in the office, late one night." Esther ignored the shiver moving down her spine.

Cullen glanced toward the door down the aisle. "A few months ago, right?"

"Yes. Back before Christmas of last year. A heart attack." Why was he staring at her like that? And how did he know so much about her father?

"And you're sure it was a heart attack?"

Growing more perturbed, she said, "Yes."

"Did the authorities verify that?"

"Yes. He had a history of heart problems. What are you suggesting?" Esther didn't want to discuss the details of her father's sudden death with a stranger. Uneasy, she moved away. "I really need to close up now."

Cullen glanced toward the front. "Please listen to me. Your

father and I corresponded in detail about this diamond. Right before he died, he hinted that he might know its location. He planned to give me the details. But I never heard from him again and then I found out about his death. Did he ever mention anything about this to you?"

Angry now, Esther moved away. "You should have mentioned that you knew my father. But since you didn't, I'll fill in the blanks for you. Even though he did extensive research on it, I don't know anything about this diamond. My father enjoyed theories, but he never actually went about trying to find the chocolate diamond. I think you need to leave, Mr. Murphy."

She started toward the door.

Cullen grabbed his hat and bag and followed her. "Do you have another showcase? A hidden one? Or a safe where you keep the really good stuff?"

She did. But she wasn't about to open it up to the likes of him, especially when she didn't have her assistant here to watch the shop and serve as a protector. Besides, this man was too demanding and nosy. He made her uncomfortable. Chills chased the cold sweat running up and down her backbone.

"I don't have the diamond you're searching for," she said, turning to hold the door open for him. "My father never mentioned finding it, so even if he did discover the diamond, as I said, I don't have any information on it. I don't even know if it's real. I'm sorry you had to come all this way for nothing."

He didn't move to leave. "I have some of your father's letters in my bag. I thought you might like to have them."

Esther's heart crashed and thumped. Her father, a faithful man and the only parent she'd ever known since her mother died during Esther's birth, had made his living here in this dusty old shop, but he'd also had an adventurer's soul. And yet he'd never traveled afar, because he couldn't leave this shop or his daughter. Esther knew this, even if Jefferson Carlisle had never once said the words out loud.

She cleared her throat. "He used to read to me every night, grand adventures. *Gulliver's Travels, Sinbad,* Homer's *Odyssey, The Three Musketeers,* and *Treasure Island,* of course." She looked at the battered bag, remembering how he used to call her a princess. A princess who lived in the white swamp. She pushed away the memories. "I would imagine his letters, even if technical, would be very colorful."

"And very thorough," Cullen replied. "I had to meet the daughter he loved so much."

And find a diamond worth millions.

Maybe she had jumped to the wrong conclusion about him. Esther stood there, pondering what to do or say. She wasn't used to a handsome stranger rushing into her shop, demanding rare fifty-carat diamonds. But she had heard her father mention the Levi-Lafitte Diamond over and over again. And always with that faraway look of adventure and intrigue in his eyes. He'd seemed frantic and obsessed with it in his last few months on earth. What if he had discovered something right before his death but hadn't had a chance to tell her? Why had he never mentioned Cullen Murphy?

"Maybe you can come back tomorrow. If my father had the diamond or even knowledge of where it might be, he never indicated it to me." Jefferson Carlisle hadn't talked much about anything else other than business. Not even to his daughter. Besides, this particular diamond would be worth millions. Why would her father keep something so significant from his only daughter?

Cullen Murphy rocked on his worn boots. "I was hoping I could poke around tonight. If I find the diamond, I'm willing to make a deal with you regarding its worth."

"I don't allow poking around in my shop after hours, Mr. Murphy. And if I did have that diamond, it wouldn't be for sale."

His eyebrows dipped at that declaration. He put his hands on his hips, his gaze sweeping the shop with the sharpness of an eagle. "It is rather hard to see everything in this grow-ing dusk. But you seem to have some wonderful collections. I'd like to go through those toy soldiers, too. And I see you also have a nice gun collection. I suppose I *could* come back tomorrow."

Glad he seemed reasonable, Esther nodded. "We keep the low lights on all night. And the alarm."

That made him grin. "Warning me against coming back later?"

"Just letting you know I have several security measures."

He leaned close, his inky eyes swallowing her in a blue haze. "I'm well aware of your security measures."

He had his nerve. As if she'd let him take a huge hunk of an historical diamond, anyway. A gem that rare and large would be worthy of some serious negotiations. Esther could barter and bargain with the best of them, so if he thought he could fool her, he was badly mistaken.

"Why don't you come back tomorrow then? My assistant, Ted Dunbar, will be here, so I'll be able to leave the front and help you. That way, you can spend all day 'poking around,' as you put it."

"Thank you," Cullen said, a look of relief washing his features. His eyes turned smoky. "It was nice to finally meet you." He turned to leave then pivoted and dug inside his bag. "Here, the letters. This isn't all of them, but he men-tions you a lot in this batch." Pulling out a leather pouch tied with a string, he handed it to her. "Your father adored you, you know."

"I adored him, too." Esther took the letters, her fingers touching on the leather. "Thank you."

The bundle smelled of leather and musk. Moved to tears at the thought of reading her father's words, she stiffened and waited for Cullen to step out, then went to lock the door once again, her brief brush with mystery and intrigue over for now. "I'll see you tomorrow, maybe."

But Cullen suddenly shoved his way back in and grabbed her so fast, she spun around like a ballerina in a music box.

Giving him a push, she shouted, "What are you doing?"

He balanced her against his chest. His warm, broad chest. "We have a bit of trouble, luv."

"Trouble?" Esther couldn't comprehend what the man was talking about. She was too caught up in the worldly, earthy smell of him and his travel clothes. Heady stuff, this. Rich and dark and spicy—and dangerous.

Cullen kept moving her ahead of him. "Men, two of them. Big, ugly, mean men, coming up the street. I'm pretty sure they have guns."

That got her attention. She pulled away and quickly locked the door.

Cullen tugged her toward the back before she could set the alarm. "We need to hide."

"What? Why?" Her voice lifted with each tug of his hand. Clutching tightly to her father's letters, she asked, "What do they want?"

He shot a covert look over his shoulder. "Me." Then he whispered close, "Oh, and they might be looking for that diamond, too."

TWO

"What do you mean, you?" And the diamond? "I don't have that diamond."

Esther glanced back and saw the shadows outside the door. Big, hulking shadows. Could this day get any worse?

Cullen shoved her toward the back. "I'll explain later."

She ground her loafers to a halt. "No, now. I can call the police, you know." To prove that point, she reached inside the deep pocket of her flared skirt and pulled out her cell phone.

"No police. Not a good idea," Cullen replied, dragging her with him in spite of her feet being practically glued to the floor. "This is too big, too dangerous. We can't trust anyone."

She had a finger on the Nine when the banging on the door started. "I won't let them ruin my shop."

He pulled her into a dark hallway and tugged her close, his breath fanning her now-disheveled hair. "Darlin', you won't be able to stop them. And better a ruined shop than the alternative."

"But—"

"Listen to me, Esther. Some very dangerous people know about the chocolate diamond and they think your father had it. If I hadn't reached you first, it would be even worse, trust me. And you do need to trust me, understand?"

Trust him? He'd come here demanding a diamond that she figured didn't even exist, and now he had thugs looking for him and this alleged diamond and he wanted her to trust him instead of the police? Right.

"I don't know you and I've had enough." She tried to punch numbers. "I won't stand for this."

He took her phone away and tucked it into one of his many pockets. "No police. That could make things much worse."

"Why? Because you're actually a criminal and you lied to me about everything?"

He winced. "I used to be a criminal, but I'm reformed now. And technically, I haven't lied about anything."

She didn't believe him. Except for the *criminal* part. She could imagine him doing bad things, very bad things. He had that kind of look about him. Half treasure hunter, half pirate. All male.

"I won't go anywhere with you," she said, wondering about the lesser of two evils. Should she pray for intervention or distraction?

He sighed and held her up like a rag doll, his eyes level with hers. "I don't have time to argue with you. If you don't do as I say, they will either torture you or kill you. Or both."

The banging ended and the sound of crashing glass took its place.

"What's it going to be, Esther?"

She stared up at the man holding her, her heart beating so fast she thought she was having an attack.

"What's really going on here?" she shouted, her fingers digging into his shirt.

"More than I can explain right now," he replied. "Now let's get out of here."

She heard the splintering of the two-hundred-year-old door and closed her eyes, willing this dream to be over. But it wasn't. Cullen was still there when she opened her eyes. And she heard footsteps rushing through the shop.

"Do you have a back entrance?" he said, still dragging her

along the wall, bumping her against old picture frames and antique wall sconces.

Apparently, he'd made her decision, Esther thought with each jump in her pulse. She was going with Cullen.

"Yes." She bobbed her head, then motioned to a hallway beyond a door on the left. "It leads to the courtyard."

"Okay, let's go."

Esther heard more crashing and then chairs scraping with irritating force, followed by drawers being opened and dropped. The shattering of precious crystal almost caused her to run back to save her place of business.

"Don't," Cullen said, his gaze hitting her with a warning.

She hated the tears that burned at her eyes, but this was her life. Her only life. Her father had worked hard to build a solid reputation in the antiques and collectibles world and Esther had vowed to carry on that tradition. She'd given up almost everything else to hold on to this showroom. If she lost this place, where would she go? Certainly not to Great-Aunt Judith's in Lake Charles. That woman might be her only living relative, but she was ancient and mean and she lived in a trailer with six cats.

They reached the door. Esther shoved the letters into Cullen's hands so she could get to her keys.

"Hurry," Cullen said, pushing her to unlock it. He put the letters in his big knapsack. "We need to hide somewhere." Then he pulled out an intricate box and quickly opened it to reveal an exquisite pistol. "I bought this next door, but it's not loaded." He shrugged. "I'm guessing here, but I think they'll probably shoot at us. They won't kill us. They'll want to question us about the diamond. But we can bluff our way out with this if we have to. Only use this gun if something happens to me. And make them think it's loaded."

They had real guns and he wanted her to fake her way out of this with an empty six-shooter?

"This cannot be happening," Esther kept repeating, her key

ring jingling, her body shaking with each thump and crash. "Not to me. I follow rules, Mr. Murphy. Rules."

"Forget the rules," Cullen said, his Irish accent on hard-drive. "And lock this door behind us. Right now, we need to find a way to stay alive."

She secured the door, knowing it wouldn't matter but it might buy them some time. Then she motioned to her studio. "We can hide in there. It has another entrance. To St. Peter Street. We might be able to get away and double back."

He guided her to the old garage. "It looks rickety," he said on a sharp breath. "And we don't have time to get to the exit door. They'll spot us."

"Do you have any other ideas?" She heard more precious items breaking, more doors slamming, then the echo of excited voices. "Maybe we can make a run for it."

"Let's go," he said, his hand on her arm. "We might be able to wait them out or we can take the side-street exit."

He hurried her into the growing dusk but kept her close to the courtyard wall, without regard for her bougainvillea vine or her beloved ferns and begonias.

She didn't know about him, but she wasn't waiting around. She intended to get away from those goons and Cullen Murphy, too. And she *would* go to the police. Her shop was open now and vulnerable to looters. She had to do something.

Esther tried the door of the studio, her hands shaking. Cullen put his hands over hers, the heat of his skin shocking her. "Which key?"

She looked down at the big ring. "The silver one with the fleur-de-lis," she said on a scattered whisper.

Cullen grabbed the key ring and fumbled with the door. They heard voices and more shouting and crashing.

Then across the way, the heavy back door to her storeroom and attached miniwarehouse crashed apart like a tinker toy. Esther squeezed her eyes shut, waiting for the bullets.

But Cullen had her inside the studio and back behind a work bench before she could catch her next breath.

"Don't move," he said, his body guarding her, hiding her, holding her. "Don't even breathe."

"That won't be a problem," she said between gasps. "I'm too scared."

Even though she didn't know the man and even though he'd brought trouble to her door, she said a silent prayer, thanking God that Cullen was here and blocking her from these people.

They waited, crouched on the floor, the shapes of her whimsical, mismatched sculptures all around them looking more like gargoyles and monsters than art. To calm herself, Esther thought back over her day. What about that nice couple from Illinois? Patt and Dave, yes. They loved antiques and also collected ceramics and glass, and had purchased several pieces, including a set of Roseville Bleeding Heart vases and an exquisite Depression glass pink bowl.

Esther heard voices followed by heavy footsteps. She was back inside the nightmare. So she prayed. Over and over.

Cullen tightened his grip. "Hold on."

She did, her hand grasping his arm, taking in his strength. She had to depend on him to help her through this. But later, she'd let him have it with both barrels.

I'm strong, she thought, fear and shock making her want to giggle. *I've managed to survive and keep on going, even when I've had no one. Well, not exactly no one. I have Aunt Judith at least. And sweet Mr. Reynolds and his wife from next door. And Harold the lonely saxophone player down the street. I have Ted, of course.* Her one loyal employee and occasional dinner companion. Ted had been sick today, but he sure wouldn't be happy come tomorrow. Their insurance would skyrocket. Ted had been her father's right-hand man. He always focused on the bottom line.

Esther prayed while she waited. *Please, Lord, let this be a dream. Let me wake up, right now.*

The footsteps drew closer and from her vantage point inside the old workroom, Esther could see that the two men searching for them did indeed have guns. Ugly, skinny-barreled guns. She prayed Cullen's sleek but ancient weapon would at least scare them.

"They have silencers," he said on a whisper, probably to remind her of the danger. Then he looked at the empty gun in his hand. "While I love this sweet Remington, I think I'm gonna need to use my 9 mm SIG-Sauer. It's fully loaded."

The man had two guns? She supposed that was a good thing. Or maybe that confirmed that he was truly a bad person.

Cullen put a finger to his mouth to warn her and then he placed the Remington back in its case and set it out of the way. She watched as he pulled out another gun and did a few clicks and loads. What all did he have in that travel bag?

Because she had no one else to turn to right now, Esther stayed there beside him, her gaze hitting on the banana-leaf fronds swaying in the humid air, her nostrils taking in the sweet scents of jasmine and wisteria, mingled with the faint scent of perspiration. She heard the steady trickle of water coming out of the twisted metal fountain sculpture she'd made three years ago. Her courtyard had always been her haven.

Now she'd never look at it in the same way again.

The men kept coming until they'd reached the glass-paned doors of the studio. One of them, looking like a hulking giant, pressed his big nose to the door and stared in. Esther hissed, but Cullen held her tightly against him behind the big sturdy work bench, as if his body would keep her invisible. She found that rather endearing in spite of her wobbly heart and weak knees.

"Hey, Murphy, you in there?"

"They speak," she said on a low, trembling whisper. "And, surprise, they know you."

"Yes, they know me," he said, bobbing his head. "They want the diamond. Must have followed me across the globe. As if I'd hand it over to Hogan and his men."

Hogan. Why did that name sound familiar? Esther closed her eyes, wishing for her hot tea. Wishing this hot diamond hunter shielding her would go away. But not until he made those bad guys go away, too.

Tugging at his shirt, she asked, "Who is Hogan?"

He shoved the Remington case at her. "I'll explain later."

When the other man rushed to the door and shook the knob, Cullen turned toward her and opened the case. "Remember, this might buy you some time. Where is the street entrance?"

She motioned with her head, then whispered, "Behind us to the left."

"It's locked?"

"Of course."

"We need a distraction."

He glanced around and saw her blow torch.

Esther's gaze followed him. "Oh, no. You can't do that."

"I can and I will, to save your life."

And then, he was up and like a gunslinger, swinging around in a poetic kind of warrior way to grab her blow torch and wield it high in front of him.

While the doors to her studio burst apart and fell away like shattered memories.

Cullen knew she was scared, but he needed Esther to help him get them out of this situation. "Run for the door," he shouted at the same time he started firing.

The two men broke apart and dropped down with guns blazing, but Cullen kept advancing, zigzagging behind tables and half-finished sculpture pieces. Somehow through the haze of darkness and with the blessing of surprise on his side, he managed to stay out of the line of fire.

He had the SIG-Sauer in one hand and the blow torch in the other. He triggered the gun, marveling at the way it hissed in his right hand. The blow torch did the same in his left, sending a white-hot heat toward the two bumbling thugs. He wasn't really aiming for anyone in particular. He mainly wanted to scare these two so Esther could get away. Which was probably what she'd been hoping for all along. She'd be gone in a flash, but at least she'd be safe. Or she might use his unusable, unloaded Remington six-shooter on him—hitting him over the head.

"Go, Esther!"

But prim little Esther surprised him.

"Not without you," she shouted, the big gun in her tiny hand.

She headed for the locked door, but instead of testing the six-shooter, she managed to find a few ceramic pots and other interesting weapons along the way. And in spite of being a little spit of a thing, the woman had an impressive aim. She heaved a pot, followed by a crude-looking knife that could only be some sort of sculpture tool. While neither made a direct hit, her projectiles did stop the two attackers from advancing. Then she lifted the Remington with both hands, as if she actually knew what she was doing. It didn't fire, of course.

This might turn out to be fun, if he didn't die.

More importantly, all fun and frolic aside, he couldn't let Esther Carlisle die. He'd made a promise to her father that he'd protect her. Cullen wasn't known for keeping promises, but this one was important to the tune of millions of dollars. It had taken him several months and a whole lot of territory to finally make it here to fulfill that promise. He wasn't about to give in so easily now.

So he shot one last flare from the blow torch and glanced back to see Esther standing at the open door, her hands frozen in place on the Remington. Then he dropped the torch and used both hands to hold the gun steady as he went after the two men.

And this time, he aimed to kill.

Esther's heart seemed to hit with all the velocity of those zinging bullets. She heard the sound of traffic and people, heard that sweet saxophone playing up near the café. She sent out a prayer that they would all be safe.

"Cullen, hurry," she called, wanting with every fiber of her being to run. The exquisite gun she held was useless, but it gave her a sense of security. Besides, she was pretty sure it could still be dangerous, even with an empty chamber.

No matter, she couldn't leave him.

And that made her more angry than frightened. Why was she willing to stand here and be killed for a man who'd crashed into her world without explanation and changed it without any apparent qualms? Because, he brought her father's letters with him. That meant for some strange reason her father had reached out to this man, had trusted him. Maybe Cullen had some answers. Answers she needed, since her father hadn't confided in her about much of anything.

Cringing as he ducked, Esther watched Cullen shooting his way across her studio. So far, so good. Then she heard sirens.

"Cullen, someone must have called the police." Mr. Reynolds, obviously. His hearing was remarkable for a seventy-year-old. And his wife, Helen, was spry and sharp and interested in the things going on around her. Esther hoped neither of them decided to pop over and investigate.

Cullen hurried to the door, then turned to fire a couple more shots. At least the two men were pinned down at the front of the studio. Probably with singed eyebrows and burning skin.

Cullen rushed her out the door and closed it tight, locking it to be double sure. Then he slipped the pistol back in the shoulder bag he'd managed to hang on to and handed her back her phone. "I think you had a call."

Shocked at how efficiently the man multitasked during a shoot-out, she gave him the extra gun and took the phone. "It's Ted. He's my bookkeeper and sales associate. He was sick today so he's probably calling to see how my day went."

Cullen did a quick scan of the nearby buildings as they headed east up St. Peter toward the Mississippi River. Off to the left the St. Louis Cathedral was bathed in the golden light of dusk. And directly across, Jackson Square teemed with tourists and locals alike. Nobody seemed to care that shots had been fired and sirens were wailing.

"What are you going to tell him?"

Esther lifted her brows, took a deep breath, then punched numbers. "That everything is fine, thank you."

But in her heart, she had a funny feeling that everything wasn't fine. In fact, holding on to the handsome, capable, daring man who'd done his best to protect her—after he'd ruined her day and her shop—she was pretty sure her life had changed forever.

And the scary part? She'd never felt more alive.

THREE

"Ted, tell the police it was a break-in. I'd locked the door but hadn't set the alarm. Two men came in and started shooting, but I ran to the back and hid in the studio. Then I managed to get away."

She heard Ted's deep exhale. "They shot at you? I can't believe this. Are you sure you're okay?"

"I'm fine," she said, trying to reassure him. "Check on Mr. and Mrs. Reynolds for me. I'm headed back there now. I'll come around front."

"Good, because I got here and the police are asking all sorts of questions. And Mr. Reynolds is talking to them right now. Of course, Miss Helen is telling anyone who'll listen that we all almost got murdered. But are you okay? I mean, really okay?"

Ted fretted about things, especially *her* health and well-being. "I'm fine but rattled. I could have stayed to fight them but they had guns and I—"

She stopped, refusing to lie, but she'd also left out the part about the handsome tomb raider who'd helped her escape, and Esther was glad of that for now. She'd have to tell Ted about that later, when her assistant wasn't about to hyperventilate. Later, when she could think straight.

Of course, if Helen Reynolds had seen Cullen, the whole city would know about him soon enough.

She hung up, then stared at Cullen. "I have to go file a police report. I can't hide this from them. This is my livelihood and I'll have to file an insurance report."

He did another scan of the area. "Okay. I get that. But we need to talk."

"Yes, I'm all ears," she retorted. "I think you have more on your travel itinerary than searching for diamonds, right?"

He didn't even bother trying to look innocent. "Yes, and I'll explain. But not here, okay? Is there someplace besides your shop where we can meet back up? Maybe somewhere I can hide out for a while?"

Esther shivered in spite of the warm night. Her clothes were dirty and rumpled, her hair falling down around her face. She wanted a bath and a cup of tea and…she wanted to wake up with her shop back intact and her brain less jumbled.

She should tell him to take a hike, but she was in this up to her neck now. And she wanted answers. "I have another place in the Garden District. My father lived over the shop, but I live in a studio apartment behind an estate house." She thought about hiding Cullen in the space over the shop, but she didn't like the idea of him snooping around up there. "My place is on Prytania Street. You can stay there until I get finished, but I'd rather not have another shoot-out."

"I promise if anyone shows up, I'll draw them away from the house," he said, his blue-gray eyes washing over her like a storm. "Will your landlord mind?

"No." She wasn't about to tell him that her friend relied on Esther's discretion. "Maybe this is a bad idea," she said. She couldn't risk anything happening to Lara's second home in the United States. "Can't you find a hotel?"

"They'd check all the hotels."

"Who are *they?* Who is Hogan?" She knew she'd heard that name before.

"Not here," he said, pulling her through the crowd. "It's too risky."

He tugged her toward the corner, then glanced into the crowd. "They must have split once they heard the sirens. I'll shadow you back to your shop, then I'll find my way to your other house. Do you have a key?"

She gave him the address and told him where to find the spare key. "I have an alarm, but it's one of those kind that alerts me, not the police or a security company," she explained. Then she whispered the code. Grabbing him by the arm, she leaned close. "Cullen, don't make me regret this."

As if sensing her concerns, he reached into his bag and brought out the small worn leather pouch again. "Your father's letters. You can read them later, but for now that's all the proof you need in order to trust me."

Esther touched the rough dark leather, the warmth from Cullen's body still on it. "Thank you—again." She noticed the street sign at the corner of St. Peter and Royal. "We can part here. The shop is right up there."

He nodded. "I'll watch until I see you with the police. I'll be waiting, Esther. It's not safe for you here alone."

He looked as if he didn't want to leave. "Go," she said, her heart flooding with gratitude. But her head still buzzed with questions. So she headed toward Carlisle Collectibles and braced herself for what she might find.

And she prayed Cullen would make it to the Garden District safely.

"Are you sure you're all right?"

Esther rubbed her temple and nodded at Ted. "Other than a couple of scratches and getting hot and dirty, I'm okay. I have a headache, but I'm fine, really."

Mr. Reynolds stood outside the office door. "Esther, I heard all the shooting. 'Bout scared the daylights outta me. I called the police right away."

"Thank you," she told the elderly merchant. "I'm so glad you didn't get caught in the cross fire." Then she glanced beyond him. "Where's Miss Helen?"

"Oh, she went back to our shop to tell our employees what happened and caution them. She saw several strangers hanging around today."

Esther's heart skipped a beat on that one. "Really? Did she talk to the police?"

"She tried, but she didn't have enough of a description to really help, I'm afraid. She wasn't wearing her bifocals."

Esther couldn't stop the sigh of relief that washed over her.

Ted watched Esther with his intense brown eyes, *his* bifocals and spiky dirty-blond hair intact. Ted was a worrier. He fretted about money. He paced when they didn't get many customers. He was always rearranging things and searching out every nook and cranny to make sure they could make a good impression on their devoted, long-standing clients. But he was good at his job and he had always been devoted to Esther and her father.

He sank down in a chair across from her after Mr. Reynolds left. "Tired of all the questions from the police?"

Esther leaned back in the red leather armchair, her gaze moving over the uniformed officers roaming around the shop. "They're doing their jobs."

The intruders had broken most of the items along the main aisle. A few vases and knickknacks, some picture frames and lamps—some expensive and some for show. They'd overturned chairs and ripped out the stuffing, and shot open some of the cabinet locks. And they'd tried without success to break the shatter-proof glass surrounding the estate jewelry. They'd wanted something they couldn't find in that case, however.

Cullen and that diamond, no doubt.

Thus proving what Cullen had told her. At least they had not found the safe and her secret stash of exquisite jewels. Good thing, since the Levi-Lafitte Diamond wasn't there, either.

"They destroyed the office," she said, knowing she sounded redundant since the desk drawers were open and gaping and most of her papers and books were tossed to the far walls. She wanted to get back to Cullen so she could get to the bottom of this mess. But sitting here, she couldn't help but notice the broken frame that covered the only picture her father had kept of him with her mother. According to her father, Marilyn had been five months pregnant with Esther when the picture was taken.

Ted pushed at his glasses and coughed. Then he picked up the shattered picture and set it back on the desk. "A break-in. Esther, I'm so sorry you had to deal with this."

Mr. Reynolds came back, surprising her with a bottle of water. "Here, honey. Drink this."

Esther took the offering, glad she had people who cared about her. "Thank you." She smiled up at both men. "I'm okay, really. We've been blessed. We've never been robbed before."

Esther glanced out into the shop, watching as uniformed officers and plainclothes detectives went about their work and instructed the crime scene investigators. She'd gone round and round with the first officer on the scene to get Ted and Mr. Reynolds in the barricaded front door. They couldn't straighten things up until the crime scene people had dusted everything for prints and extracted a few bullets. Standard procedure, according to the dour officer in charge. But there wasn't much hope of finding anything that would lead them to the men who'd done this, also according to that same officer.

Like Miss Helen, Esther hadn't been able to give very much of a description, either. She might have to go into the station and look through mug shots. Not that that would help. *Big and burly* was the only way to describe those two. If they'd truly followed Cullen across the universe, they could be international criminals. And he might be, too, for that matter. But she had no idea how to explain that to the nice officers and detectives. They'd laugh if she told them about a giant ancient chocolate diamond, too.

Her father would be so disappointed in her right now. Withholding information from the police went against Carlisle standards.

"So you didn't get a good look?" Mr. Reynolds asked. He was obviously afraid the thugs would come back to finish the job. Or maybe rob him next time.

"I don't remember details," she said.

Ted patted her hand. "Maybe you'll remember something later."

"I saw two big men dressed in black and carrying guns. But I took off before they got up close. I was running for my life so I didn't stop to get a picture."

"I'm sorry, Esther." Ted plopped down on a stool near her feet, then looked up at her with those puppy-dog brown eyes. "I should have been here to protect you."

She almost laughed, hysterically. Ted was about as puny as they came. He was a sweetheart and a devoted employee, but he had severe allergies and he was terrified of everything from spiders to shoplifters. She probably would have wound up protecting him.

"No, I'm glad you weren't here," she said, meaning it. "I managed to get away and that's the important thing."

Ted didn't seem convinced. "I'll go out and see if I can help with anything." He turned to Mr. Reynolds. "Thanks for calling 911."

Esther nodded. "Yes, thank you so much. I panicked. By the time I was safe, the sirens were already wailing."

One of the officers approached her after Ted went out into the shop. "So you were closing up for the day, right?"

"Yes," she said, standing to face him. "I had one late customer who wanted to look at some jewelry, but he didn't find what he was looking for."

That was the truth. But she couldn't allow for any more information. Or should she give the police Cullen's name and description and be done with it?

Her head shouted yes, but her heart screamed no.

"Did you know this customer? Is he a regular?"

"No. He was traveling through."

The officer looked skeptical. "He could have been a front—a distraction."

Esther thought about that, but why would Cullen need to distract her? He had a gun and so did those men. They'd fired at Cullen. Had that all been a show for her? To convince her to listen to him and trust him?

"I don't know," she said, being honest on that account at least.

"Did you find anything missing from the jewel cabinets?" she asked the officer instead.

"Come see for yourself," the young officer replied. "Looks like they tried to shoot the lock, but the glass held. Must be some powerful glass."

"We have some very rare, one-of-a-kind jewels," she replied, motioning to Ted and hoping he'd go into the storage room and check the vault behind the secret wall her father had built years ago. She discreetly pointed to the storage room door.

Ted dashed away while she talked to the police. Esther studied the three main jewel cases, each ring and brooch, each elegant necklace and sparkling bracelet with matching earrings etched in her brain. "Nothing's missing that I can tell."

The officers nodded, wrote in their little notebooks, then suggested she padlock the doors for the night.

Ted came back up the aisle and helped her. "Safe is intact," he said under his breath.

One of the officers approached them. "You can call the alarm company first thing tomorrow, but for now you need to do something to protect your property."

"We can use the hurricane shutters," Ted suggested. "You know, we'll put up that plywood we used when the last big one came through, on the inside of the door. Then if we tug the shutters closed and lock them. I can sleep down in the showroom."

"No," Esther said, startling not only Ted but a nearby officer. "I don't think you should stay here tonight."

"You shouldn't stay here alone," Mr. Reynolds said from his spot near the broken doors. He hovered, worry on his aged face. "Wanna come over to our apartment?"

Esther would have, under any other circumstances. The couple attended her church and treated her like their own daughter. She could use that kind of comfort tonight. "Thanks, but no. I'm going home. I'm exhausted."

Esther had to get rid of the police and Ted before she could meet up with Cullen. She had to find out the whole story about this mess.

"I'll be fine," she said. "I'll stay at my own apartment tonight. Surely they won't go there."

"Can you call a friend?" the officer suggested.

Ted bobbed his head. "One of your church friends maybe."

She almost laughed at the irony of that. Cullen probably hadn't graced a church door his whole life. But her friend and absent landlord, Lara, was a devout churchgoer. She'd be safe in her studio at Lara's private compound. Only, Lara wasn't in the States right now. But what about Cullen Murphy? Would she be safe with him?

"I'll be okay at my place." She waited for the police to finish up, then turned to Ted. "Now we'll need the hammer, some nails and that plywood. And you know I'll need you to help me pull the storm shutters down. I always have trouble with that."

Esther had learned years ago that keeping Ted busy was the best thing for her sanity and his. He hurried to his tasks.

"I'll help," Mr. Reynolds said, hobbling to catch up with Ted, his red bow tie askew.

"Do you know of anyone who's angry with you? Or out

to do you in?" the officer in charge asked, his thick New Orleans accent sliding over the quiet office.

"No, sir."

"Have you ever seen the two men who came in here before today?"

"No, sir. Never."

He scowled, doubt clearly written all over his face. "Think hard. You might know them and not realize it."

Why did police officers always seem so jaded and cynical?

Maybe because, here in this city, they saw pretty much everything?

"I can assure you, I don't know them."

"If you remember anything else, let us know," the officer said. Then he and his men finished up their business.

Two hours later, Esther felt guilt tickling at her conscience when she finally convinced Mr. Reynolds to go home and told Ted they'd done all they could for now. They'd cleared up some of the debris and secured the doors and rechecked the inventory. The safe hadn't been touched.

"I rode my bike to work this morning, but maybe I'll take a cab home," she told Ted. At least she had her car at the carriage-house apartment.

Ted held his hands against his waist. "Want me to ride with you?"

Then she'd feel obligated to invite him in and she couldn't do that. Not tonight. "No. I'm really tired. And you're still sick from that cold. You need to rest, too."

He gave her a disappointed nod. "You'll call me if you need anything, right?"

"Of course. I promise."

Ted found her a cab, then stood on the street corner watching as the car pulled away. He waved and she turned and waved out the back window, thankful for having someone to help her through this. Had she mentioned her late-day customer to Ted? She couldn't remember. She'd have to tell him about Cullen sooner or later. Esther put that out of her mind, however.

Even though she was exhausted, she was eager to have a sit-down with Cullen Murphy and find out the real reason he'd disrupted her life.

Because things weren't adding up. He'd come to the shop searching for the diamond, but he thought the diamond could possibly be buried in the swamp. He claimed he'd corresponded with her father, yet Esther had never before seen a letter come in from Cullen. Did he have a map? Had her father sent him clues? Or had her father kept things from her, maybe even a post office box?

Her father had never once mentioned he had someone else interested in this quest for the Levi-Lafitte Diamond. But then, Jefferson Carlisle hadn't been a man of many words. He'd done his fatherly duties by teaching Esther right from wrong, reading to her from her favorite books when she was younger and spinning tales to entertain her when they were both lonely. Then he'd given her a solid art-and-history education at Tulane.

Her father had been quiet, studious and dependable. And lost in the world of antiques and rare jewels. Esther felt he would have told her of his discovery, since he did often talk about the possibility of finding the diamond. It had been a constant subject in the weeks before his death, to the point of making him ill. But he'd never once mentioned that he might have found the diamond.

What were you hiding, Father? she silently wondered. And more to the point now, what was Cullen Murphy hiding?

FOUR

Cullen watched Esther coming out the back door of the boarded-up shop, the squirrelly man who must be Ted with her. Together they worked to put a padlock on the broken door. Esther held a flashlight while Ted wrestled with the chain and lock. Cullen's first instinct was to go and help, but he was here only to make sure Esther got safely to the Garden District.

He couldn't leave her behind to the mercy of Charles Hogan's dangerous men. Those men would be back. They'd been chasing Cullen for months, but he'd always managed to shake them off. Hogan fancied himself a serious collector, but the man wouldn't know taste if it bit him in the ear. He wanted the chocolate diamond, though. That much Cullen knew. And if he knew Hogan, the man didn't just want to show off the diamond in some glassed-in display.

Hogan ran with a nefarious crowd. If he wanted the diamond, it couldn't be for good. Cullen had heard tales of gun-running and illegal weapons, maybe even drug smuggling. And now he'd brought Hogan's men right to Esther's door. It was up to him to find that diamond before they did and to protect Esther, too. Not exactly what he'd had in mind when coming to New Orleans.

The best-laid plans...

After Esther and Skinny Ted locked everything up tight, Cullen followed them out onto the street next to the on-site studio. If she planned to walk, he'd be right behind her. If Skinny planned to tag along, Cullen would be right there behind him, too.

They talked back and forth in what looked like an argumentative way and then Ted hailed a taxi and opened the door for Esther. Ted watched until she was in the cab, then reluctantly turned and hurried in the other direction.

Cullen started running to catch up. The cab stopped at the corner of St. Peter and Royal up near the square. Cullen slapped the window next to Esther.

She glanced up in fear, followed by shock, followed by dread. He had that effect on women.

"Hi," he said as he slid in beside her. "Long time, no see."

She glanced at the confused cabbie. "He's a friend. Go ahead." Then she leaned close. "You were supposed to be at the other studio. Didn't I give you directions?"

Cullen saw the fatigue in her eyes. She wasn't used to dealing with the likes of him. Her innocence made him feel bad about all the secrecy and shooting. "You gave me wonderful directions," he said, taking his hat off so he could scissor his fingers through his hair. "But I wasn't about to leave you alone back there."

"You've been—"

"Watching," he said, the one word a whisper. "I wanted to make sure you were safe."

"How nice of you." She pushed at runaway strands of silky russet-and-copper tresses. "Considering that I was all set to go home to a nice bubble bath and a good cup of Earl Grey before *you* dashed into my shop and brought thugs with you, I'd say keeping me safe is the last thing on your mind."

Ouch. Cullen held a hand to his heart. "Wow, I felt that arrow. Your aim is perfect."

She lowered her voice, her eyes flashing fire. "My aim is to make you see that you are a dangerous man. I should make you get out of this cab right now, but I want answers. I wasn't honest with the police or my assistant because I want answers, so I get first dibs on questioning you. If that diamond is out there and someone unscrupulous—besides you, of course—is after it then I have to stop them. It belongs in a museum, not in the hands of greedy people."

Her sharp, disapproving glance told him he ranked high in that category.

Now would probably not be the best time to tell her that, well, yes, he wanted the diamond all for himself. It was worth millions. Auctioned off to the highest bidder, that little bauble could bring Cullen a fortune. And that fortune could give him endless possibilities, careerwise.

But the lovely lass sitting beside him like a stiff doll wouldn't see things that way. He was in more trouble than he'd realized. He found a lady with a conscience. This could get messy.

"What a mess," she said, her words eerily echoing his thoughts. "I don't have that diamond, but thanks to you, someone thinks I might. Do you think they'll come back?"

Cullen nodded. "If they know I'm still here, yes. I'm after the diamond. They want to get to it before me. Or rather, use me to find it."

She slanted him a golden-eyed look. "Did you know those men were chasing you before or after you darkened my door?"

He cleared his throat and glanced at the traffic moving along St. Charles Avenue. "I might have suspected it a bit, luv."

"You knew," she said. "You knew and you didn't bother to warn me at all. What kind of man are you?"

He leaned in close, his whisper partly a warning and partly a suggestion. "The kind you should never let into your shop."

She should probably not let him into her apartment, either. Or her life. But he'd started this and she needed his help to finish it. So she turned at the French doors of the two-bedroom studio inside the grounds of the wedding-cake-white mansion that belonged to her friend Lara Barrington Kincade. Long and narrow and two-storied with a quaint little balcony off the top floor, the apartment had once been a carriage house. The workshop off the kitchen and bedroom used to house horses and carriages, and later, fancy cars. Now it was full of light and roomy enough to hold Esther's equipment and supplies.

Until now, Esther had loved this place. She'd always felt safe here inside the massive compound. She'd never do anything to jeopardize her friendship with Lara. But bringing Cullen Murphy here might do that.

"You get one chance, Cullen. One more chance to tell me what's going on." She opened the door and waved him inside. "I don't suffer fools easily. If I don't like what I hear, I will be forced to alert the local authorities."

Cullen looked around and smiled. "Charming."

Esther agreed, thinking, even though his gaze swept over her rather than his surroundings, surely he was referring to the apartment. "Are we clear?"

"As clear as that exquisite Irish crystal in the hutch," he said, pointing to a long display cabinet by the dining table.

"Good." Esther took a calming breath. "My friend was kind enough to let me rent this for as long as I need it. I love her quirky decorating style and how the light plays through all the windows. It's my getaway from the Quarter. It's quiet here, especially when she's in Europe. I'd like to keep it that way."

He gave her a curious nod, then stood near the white leather sofa to admire an abstract painting by a local artist. "A very generous friend."

"Yes," she retorted, her tone brooking no argument. "Part of our agreement for me to live here and keep an eye on things was discretion, one hundred percent discretion. I aim to honor that."

"Noble of you." He looked bemused but didn't press her for more details. "Friends such as you are hard to come by."

"And people like you are hard to understand."

"You have a dazzling wit about you, luv."

She grinned at that. "Sit down and I'll find us something to eat."

"I am starving," Cullen said. "I had a long flight and an even longer layover in Atlanta. American airports are as tedious as an ancient dig and not at all as exciting."

Esther took that in but decided she'd drill him after they'd both had time to catch their breaths. But instead of sitting, he paced and checked, going from window to window, his actions calculated and precise. And nerve-racking.

"You think they'll show up here?" she asked while she made turkey sandwiches and sliced fruit and cheese.

"I don't know. No one followed the taxi as far as I could tell. But all of these windows—"

"I have a good alarm system."

"They'd know how to disarm it."

"Is that your way of trying to calm me down?"

"I'm being realistic. I brought this on you, Esther. So I intend to protect you. I'm sorry."

She stopped spreading mayo and stared over the white marble counter at him. He seemed sincere, but it could be an act. "What if you were in on the whole thing?"

He glowered. "Is that what you're asking?"

She frowned. "Is that what you're trying to tell me? You did say you used to be a criminal."

He shook his head. "I wasn't in on anything. I had one purpose—to see if you had the diamond. I'm strictly legal now. I was willing to split the sale fifty-fifty, same as what I talked about with your father. But I'm not willing to see you get hurt."

She slapped bread together and slid the plate with his sandwich toward him, purposely trying to ignore the little shiver of endearment that danced down her spine. Cullen had a way of looking at her that left her unsettled and completely confused. But he needed to explain how deeply her father had been invested in finding this diamond. "Sit down and we'll talk."

After pouring them both iced tea, in two vintage crystal goblets, Esther sat across from him, her fingers playing with the fringe on the bright blue place mats. "My father always wanted to find the diamond. But he was more of a dreamer than a doer, so I find it hard to believe he actually acted on his dreams. He never quite got over my mother's death." She shrugged, pushed at her hair. "And then, he had me to deal with, of course."

Cullen drank down some tea then looked over at her. "But he loved you. You'll see that when you read his letters. He always told me if anything happened to him, to make sure you got the letters back. I think it was his indirect way of having a record of his feelings. And maybe other things." He shot her a glance that bordered on a plea.

Had her father brought Cullen here as some sort of matchmaking ploy? Or maybe so she'd have a good friend. She was alone in the world, but perfectly capable of providing for herself. She didn't need a babysitter or a bodyguard.

But maybe her father had planned on this. Maybe he'd deliberately cultivated a relationship with a handpicked companion. After all, her father had tried hard to control her every move when she was younger.

Ridiculous. Her father wouldn't have done anything so crazy. But he would have thought about the diamond and keeping her from danger. So…Cullen was her protector?

Double ridiculous.

"He never spoke about his feelings. He kept everything buried inside while he obsessed about other things." The jealousy she felt at Cullen's closeness with her father stuck in her throat, stifling her breath. She grabbed a strawberry to wash it away. "I shouldn't resent you, but I do for some reason."

"I never would have guessed," he replied, his tone soft, his eyes dark and intense with sympathy and concern. "His focus was on research and discovery, nothing more. But I do feel as if I know you already, having read those letters."

Esther felt the heat of that admission move down her body. She did not blush becomingly, but she couldn't stop the flush of warmth covering her face. Blotches of red would soon follow.

Squaring her shoulders, she asked, "What do you think you know?"

He smiled, bit into a big green grape. "I know that you love reading classic romance novels, especially rare first editions. I know that you have a keen fascination for all things old and interesting, like your parents did. I know that you wanted to be a sculpture artist and that you are, but you're tied to that antiques shop out of a sense of duty and obligation. However, you've had several very good showings, critically acclaimed exhibits where some pieces sold to a couple of very famous people, or so I've heard. Impressive."

She stiffened again. He couldn't know that one of those sculptures sat in the entryway of the main house here. *Intimate Images.* It was an abstract of love, life and joy, forged in steel and stone—the way true love was forged. Lara, a true romantic, had loved it on sight.

Esther put that out of her mind for now. "I manage to handle both my art and the shop, thank you very much."

He lifted his finger and trailed it over her knuckles, the electricity of his touch shocking her. "No need to get all testy, luv. You are, after all, noble. It's refreshing."

She used anger to cover gratitude. "Why don't you stop analyzing me and explain yourself?"

He grinned. "I did not know that talking about yourself would make you so uncomfortable."

"Well, now you do. But having you explain things to me might make me more open to discussing the intimate details of my life—which you seem to know already anyway."

He sat back on the sleek white bar stool, his aggravatingly rugged presence overshadowing the art deco kitchen. "Okay, here's the story. I was born and raised in Dublin, Ireland. I'm the middle child of three. We didn't have much growing up, but we all worked hard. My father was strict and quiet, until he drank and then he was loud and mean. My mother was loving and sweet. She's still alive. He is not. I have an older sister and a younger sister. I was always intrigued by the past, so I studied history and archaeology in college—I worked my way through college, by the way. But I fell in with a bad lot and got in a spot of trouble."

"Criminal trouble?"

"Yes. I worked for a man who had no scruples."

"But you stopped working for this man?"

He actually looked uncomfortable for a second. "Yes. It wasn't easy to get away from him, but I did. I finished college and now I'm legitimate."

"And I'm supposed to believe that?"

He let out a breath. "I'm an archaeologist. That's my life, Esther. I find things, old things, buried things. I find rare treasures and long-forgotten artifacts. I've discovered complete villages buried underneath rock and dirt, and I've found rare artifacts in caves and in the ocean. I make a good living finding and selling some of the things I discover. I lecture on college campuses and teach students how to dig and dig and dig. I want that diamond. And I've done the research to show that if your father had it, then he hid it and left enough clues for me to take up the quest."

"So you actually think he found it?"

"He hinted at that, yes. I still don't know. He was very cryptic about it. But I do believe if he didn't find it, he knew where it might be. That's why I asked you first. I thought maybe you'd at least let me see the infernal thing—and save me a lot of grief trying to figure out his letters."

Her heart felt as heavy as that aggravating diamond. "Is that why you brought me the letters? You want me to help you find clues?"

He looked guilty but had the good grace to also look sheepish. "Partly. But, beyond that, I truly wanted you to have them too, as a memento of your father."

"When you're done with them and with me, you mean. Then I can have them as a memento."

There went that sheepish look again. "I need your help, Esther. But I won't get you killed in the process."

Esther huffed an irritated breath to hide the deep disappointment cresting inside her heart. "I told you I don't know anything and I'm not hiding the diamond. He never mentioned any of this to me. He mused about the diamond, discussed endless scenarios, but he never told me he'd found it."

"Probably to protect you."

"Probably because he kept his treasures to himself. Even if he had found the diamond, and even if he had told me about it, do you honestly believe I'd hand it over to you?"

"I thought we could negotiate a swap or a price at least. As I said earlier, your father and I had a partnership of sorts. We agreed to split everything evenly."

A partnership? He only wanted the diamond so he could make an obscene amount of money. And he was willing to barter with her in order to reach that end.

Again, her heart did a thudding drop, much the way a diamond might feel if it was flung away. Was he using her?

Of course he was here for the diamond and the money. Nothing more. It didn't surprise her, but it sure did sting.

Deciding to sting back, she said, "Sorry, but the trail is cold. My father loved to imagine what might happen if he could find the diamond, but I think he was afraid to try. Because of me. He always put me first, even when he didn't want to."

And no one else would ever do that. She needed to remember that.

"You don't know that he loved you, but you should."

She hated the sympathy, the pity, in Cullen's eyes even as his words touched her. She'd been doing fine in her own little world. Now, here he sat, all powerful and all man, like some hero out of a comic book, trying to convince her that her father loved her, trying to convince her that she was needed.

She refused to let him get the best of her with those midnight eyes and that wonderfully delightful accent.

"Are you finished?" she asked, not necessarily referring to the food.

"Yes, thank you."

Esther got up and removed their dinner dishes. "I'll make coffee. I have brownies."

Then she turned to face Cullen. "I want you to tell me about the people who tried to kill us tonight. Obviously, they think you and I know more about this cursed diamond than we actually do. Or maybe you know more and you're not telling me. I don't know what to believe at this point, but you're here now and I have to go with that. I need to know if I'm still in danger and…what you propose to do about that."

FIVE

Good question. Cullen wasn't sure what he was going to do next. His purpose had changed. He'd saved those letters, studying them, wondering at times if Esther's father might be on to something, or simply mad. When he'd realized Jefferson Carlisle might have taken the location of the diamond to his grave, Cullen had started out with a plan to come to New Orleans, visit with Esther long enough to charm her in hopes that she'd trust him and thus show him the diamond. Then he'd planned to make her an offer she couldn't refuse. And even though he'd technically promised her father he'd watch after her, Cullen had figured that would be in the form of an email here and there, an occasional letter or random text every now and then. Not an actual protection-detail kind of watch. He'd hoped she'd have the diamond and that she'd be eager to make a large sum of money. He'd in turn sell it to the highest bidder and split half with her—and that would be the end of that. While he'd been intrigued and enchanted by her loving father's description of Esther, he'd never planned to actually like the woman.

Or to be so hugely attracted to her.

This presented all kinds of problems.

Cullen hadn't thought much beyond the diamond. Nor had he figured Hogan's henchmen would find him so soon. Did they have a GPS attached to him? He'd been very careful in planning his itinerary. Besides, he always checked for bugs. Espionage came with the territory when one dealt with price-less artifacts. And when one used to work for the very man hunting the same priceless artifact. Would he ever shake the nastiness of having worked for Charles Hogan?

"I'm waiting," Esther said from across the room. She'd been frozen there like Lot's wife, watching the coffee drip.

Cullen let out a sigh and studied her. She looked rather charming even in that rigid state while she held herself to-gether with her arms at her midsection. Her hair had long ago let go of the constraints from the tight knot piled around her neck. Now it fell in russet-and-gold waves around her face, leaving just enough caught in the intricate emerald-crusted hair clamp to make him long to let it loose.

She dressed like a schoolmarm—all skirts and flats and twisted scarves—but he imagined she could be a regular beauty in a green evening gown to match that hair ornament. He had a sudden flash of holding her in his arms and danc-ing a sweet waltz with her.

She turned at that very moment, her eyes locking on him. Cullen lost his breath. There was a lioness lurking behind the schoolmarm facade.

"The coffee is ready," she said on a winded rush of breath. "I'll…get the brownies."

"Of course." He tried to stand, then gave up and sat back down. What was the matter with him? He'd never been weak at the knees before. Ever. Shouldn't have eaten that sandwich on the plane. Must have given him an upset stomach.

"Are you all right?" she asked after handing him a pris-tine white plate with a rich-looking chocolate brownie in the center.

"Yes. No. Jet lag. I'm exhausted."

"I can only imagine. Watching your back must be a con-stant chore."

She passed the cream with a smile.

Cullen took the coffee she offered him, but he didn't need the cream. He ate the brownie, however, out of nervousness. It was moist and dark and full of nuts.

He was beginning to think he was full of nuts, too.

"Wonderful. This is exactly what I needed."

Esther nibbled at her own slice. "Those men, Cullen?"

His appetite disappeared with the last crumb, making him feel sick to his stomach again. What had he done, bringing such ruthless monsters to her door?

"Charles Hogan," he said, his coffee cup in his hand. "You might have heard that name."

Her dark eyebrow lifted. "The Charles Hogan? The Charles Hogan who happens to be one of the most powerful men in all of Louisiana, possibly all of the earth?"

"The very one." Cullen took a sip of the strong coffee. "One of the richest, most powerful men in the world. He believes he should rule the world. And because he does rule so much of your fair city, he wants the Levi-Lafitte chocolate diamond to support that effort."

"My father had dealings with Mr. Hogan. But I always thought it involved antique furniture and estate jewelry."

"I think they both had their eye on that diamond from the beginning."

She didn't flinch. Instead, she seemed to stand tall across the counter from him, the lioness shining through again. "So Mr. Hogan—he'd kill for it?"

"Yes. Without any qualms."

She went pale. "And you believe he sent those men?"

"Most certainly. He's cornered me before. He thinks I can find the diamond. And he's one of the reasons I started corresponding with your father." He wanted to say more, but held back.

"Did you put my father in danger?"

"No, no." At least he prayed he hadn't. But he couldn't be sure. "I wanted information from someone I could trust.

I stumbled across your father's name when I verified that it might be located here in Louisiana. Your father had written an article about it in *Louisiana Life* magazine and I got a hit on the internet. After I researched your father, I got in touch with him and I realized he really wanted to find the diamond."

She leaned into the sparkling white stone. "Maybe I do need to read my father's letters right now. He obviously had a whole secret life I wasn't aware of."

Cullen put down his empty coffee cup. "I believe he left clues, Esther. Clues that only you can decipher."

Looking confused, she said, "But why send them to you?"

"To keep people off the trail, to keep the danger away from you."

"And yet you came here looking for me?"

"Yes, you and the diamond. I admit my intentions weren't all that honorable, but I have my reasons for being here now."

"Really?" Her sarcasm shouted at him.

"I'm sorry," he said, meaning it.

Cullen prided himself on not having a conscience. Fretting over things left everything messy and incomplete. Falling for burnished-haired women made that even worse. But Esther—how could he hurt her? Jefferson Carlisle had been a correspondent and close acquaintance for years now. And through Jefferson's many letters, Cullen had come to admire the man's only daughter.

On paper, she sounded fascinating.

In person, she was, oh, so much more.

Directness was apparently one of her best attributes. "You're sorry only because you got caught."

She had no idea how true that statement was, but he couldn't tell her the complete truth. Not yet.

"I'm not caught," he said on a defensive note. "I've outsmarted men like Charles Hogan for most of me life, luv." He'd outsmarted a lot of pretty women, too. But this one might prove to be a tough cookie.

She removed the emerald clip and shook out all of that luxurious hair. "And do you enjoy outsmarting people?"

Cullen suddenly felt *caught*. The woman practically *knew* all of his moves. He'd never before been in this kind of snare. "I…uh…enjoy the thrill of the hunt, so to speak. I enjoy finding undiscovered treasure."

And he'd certainly stumbled upon one, looking at her.

She fingered her hair out of her face, causing it to cascade like dark golden silk over her shoulders. Giving him another direct stare, she said, "You're one of those kind, the kind who has to be first at everything. The kind who conquers and pilfers and leaves things ugly, ruined and destroyed, right?"

Was she asking for confirmation? Or a warning?

"I wouldn't call myself that callous. I clean up after myself."

She turned to stare out into the moonlight. "It's not what you might clean up that scares me, Cullen. It's what you might leave behind."

Then she whirled and started gathering dishes, her disapproval of him palpable.

Obviously, she wasn't referring to holes in the earth and caves stripped of treasures.

Had he left behind some broken hearts? Probably. But he didn't plan on doing that this time. He didn't dare even think beyond getting that diamond. Nothing else mattered.

But he knew in his hardened heart that Esther did matter.

Esther Carlisle was way beyond his pay grade. He couldn't afford the woman. Because she was one of those kind—the kind who wanted romance and forever-after, the kind who wanted commitment and contentment all tied up in a nice little package. He'd need to remember that, think about that, each time he thought about kissing her or running his hands through that amazing hair.

He needed to find a way to tell her that he used to work for Charles Hogan and that the man had been chasing him since the day he'd walked away. He needed to tell her that this diamond would salvage his reputation, would bring him redemption, would finally help him shed the last of Charles Hogan's nasty hold on him.

He wanted to explain everything, but she finished tidying up and put her hands on her hips. "I'm tired. I'm going to my room. I'll read the letters and make notes. Tomorrow, we can compare. If you want that diamond so badly, then go for it. I don't want it for myself, but I'd like you to consider this if you find it. Please, Cullen? It belongs in a museum, so everyone can enjoy its beauty and understand its history. It has possible religious meaning and significance. I won't profit from that. I can't. But I'm thinking you can and you will. Just think about what I'm asking before you rush out and make a horrible mistake, please?"

Cullen sat there, still and quiet. She was asking the impossible. "I can't make that kind of promise."

She nodded. "Then we have a problem." She motioned to the hallway. "The guest bedroom and bath are that way. You'll find everything you need in the linen closet. The alarm already reset itself after I locked the door when we came in. We should be safe for the night."

With that, she turned like a queen and pivoted off to the other side of the house. Away from him.

Esther pulled her lightweight cotton robe tightly together and tied it. With a cup of tea in hand, she sank down on the chaise lounge in her bedroom then picked up the leather pouch she'd placed on the side table earlier. Did she dare read these letters? Seemed she didn't have much of a choice. She highly doubted she'd get any more information out of Cullen.

She'd rather read the letters than be in the same room with that man. He made her feel off-centered and disoriented. Esther didn't like those feelings. She didn't like being used, either.

She'd opened the pouch when her cell buzzed. Grabbing it from the table, Esther saw Ted's name and number. He'd already left several messages.

"Are you okay?"

"I'm fine," she said, too tired to explain. "I've set the alarm and now I'm going to read awhile then go to bed."

"Esther, you promised you'd call me."

"I know. I got busy and then time slipped by. I'm fine, really. I have a state-of-the-art alarm system here."

"Okay. But you call me if you need anything, you hear?"

"I will. Stop worrying and get some rest. We'll have a lot to deal with come Monday."

"They'll probably never catch those goons."

"I know. But I've learned my lesson. I'll be more careful next time."

"That reminds me—didn't you say you had one last customer?"

Esther sat up, wishing Ted didn't have a memory for details. "Yes, but he left."

And dear Lord, forgive me for that lie.

"So he couldn't help us identify those men. I thought maybe he might have seen something."

"No, he was just looking. Passing through. The police took statements from the nearby merchants. But none of them actually saw anything. They heard shots being fired."

She said good-night, her mind whirling. She didn't like withholding things from Ted. Since her father's death, he'd been her friend and helper. She depended on him for so much.

And he so much wanted her to lean on him even more.

But she wasn't attracted to Ted in that way. Dating wasn't high up on her list, since she always managed to wind up with either losers or demanders. She didn't like demands, and the ones who seemed like losers needed some proper training. Esther didn't have time to train anyone these days.

She thought about Cullen Murphy. Definitely more of a demander and definitely not trainable. A whole different breed. His accent was like a delicious melody that played over and over in her mind. His eyes fascinated her. So deep and dark, like a cave begging to be explored. He'd seen things, done things that she'd only dreamed about. But being attracted to the man didn't make this right. Even if they could find the diamond, she couldn't let Cullen take it, no matter the amount of money he offered her.

"Help me understand, Lord," she whispered into the night. Maybe that was why her father had never pursued the diamond to the end. Jefferson Carlisle would have been torn between duty and greed, but she had to believe duty would have won out with her father. He'd left Esther that legacy and she intended to honor it.

Not so much with Cullen Murphy.

She looked down at the bundle then opened the first letter. It was dated five years back. Her father and Cullen had been corresponding that long? And why not by email? Carlisle Collectibles did a lot of their business these days online and over the phone. Ted had updated their website last year. Yet, her father had always preferred the old-fashioned way of communicating. Letters made sense for him.

This did explain why Esther had never noticed the correspondence. She'd been at Tulane five years ago. He must have dealt with this while she was away during the week and sometimes even on weekends. But why? Had he been lonely, seeking someone to converse with, if only on paper? Had he been flattered by Cullen's interest?

Knowing her old-fashioned, impeccable father, Esther figured he'd rather enjoyed writing the letters by hand. Her father had been a stickler for manners and traditions. Esther moved her fingers over the dark ink, immediately recognizing her father's trademark bold, scrawling handwriting.

Dear Mr. Murphy:

What a pleasure to have such an enthusiastic collector with whom to discuss the Levi-Lafitte chocolate diamond. Diamonds in general are the subject of great <u>folklore</u> and legends, some of which are based on truth. The chocolate diamond is no exception. It is a much-talked-about gem. When first discovered, chocolate- and topaz-colored diamonds were considered inferior. Nature allows the nitrogen atoms to be spaced so that they absorb the greens and blues usually in white diamonds. This is what makes the chocolate a somewhat drab brown. But in the right light, they are incredibly beautiful.

Of course, long ago it was believed that if one <u>swallowed</u> a diamond, one would die because the rocks were poisonous. The poison rumors ran amok to keep workers from <u>stealing</u> from the mine owners. Ironic, since every dig certainly meant someone was stealing from the earth. In the case of the chocolate diamond, <u>swallowing</u> fifty carats might prove to be too much for any man!

Esther immediately noticed all the exclamation points and underlining of certain words. Her father wrote much more vividly than he'd ever talked. Or at least, he'd never been this vivid when talking to her. But, she remembered with a stab of sadness, he'd told her vivid tales of grand adventures, reading in his precise, knowledgeable voice, each word, each enunciation clear and firm and told with a gentleman's cultured Southern accent. How she missed hearing her father's voice.

The letter went on about the history of the chocolate diamond, with reference to the Twelve Tribes of Israel and how the Levi tribe had a high priest who might have possibly worn this particular diamond on his robe.

Esther skimmed over the details since she knew this by

heart. She'd never realized how serious her father must have been about finding the infamous diamond. How long had he plotted and researched and schemed in hopes of finding this treasure? He had probably also been searching for the perfect partner to help him. Well, he'd certainly found one in Cullen Murphy.

Perfect in every way. And a bit too greedy for Esther's taste. Greedy and with a criminal background. Reformed now? She doubted that. And the man was sleeping down the hall. Was he thinking about his secrets while he dreamed of that diamond?

Wide-awake now, Esther checked the dates on the other letters. Years of correspondence lay in her lap, at least three or four letters per year. Maybe Cullen was right. Maybe these letters would help her to understand Jefferson Carlisle more. Eager to finish this one and read another, Esther forgot her lukewarm tea, and instead focused on the letters again.

Then her father's words became more personal:

I have dreamed of being a great adventurer. But I have my own adventure right here in New Orleans. I can plot and calculate where Lafitte possibly buried some of his <u>stolen</u> treasure and I believe the Levi-Lafitte Diamond is <u>now</u> somewhere in Louisiana, but I dare not venture out into the unforgiving swamps to prove that theory. You see, I have a daughter whom I love dearly. Esther is a bright, engaging young woman and a talented <u>artist</u> and even though she is an adult now, I still worry about her. She is my true treasure. If something were to happen to me, she'd be all alone. I can't risk that. But that's my concern, not yours. Perhaps you might be interested in hearing more about the clues I've gathered? Maybe we could meet in person to discuss this. I'm afraid I'm tied to my shop for now, but if you're interested in com-

*ing to New Orleans, we could sit down and discuss the
details. I think you'll find my research to be fascinating.*

Her father had invited Cullen to come to New Orleans!
Had he been hoping to strike up a deal with Cullen for more
clues? Or did he have something else in mind entirely?

Such as introducing a man he obviously admired to a
daughter he claimed to treasure?

SIX

Esther felt a warm hand over her mouth.

She struggled against the chaise lounge, disoriented from sleep, letters fluttering around her like fallen leaves. Her pulse galloped against her temple as fear whirled around her in the muted darkness. Who had turned off the lamp?

"Esther, it's me."

Cullen.

So, was he going to kill her before she even had a chance to figure this out? Not if she could get to him first. She lifted her head, searching for the nearest weapon.

"Don't scream, okay? I think we have a prowler."

She didn't know whether to hit him or kiss him. She bobbed her head instead, relieved that he wasn't here to hurt her and scared because apparently someone else *was* out to get her.

He removed his hand, then lifted her off the chaise and shoved her behind him, his strength surprising her and bringing her a sense of security. Which only irritated her.

"You scared me to death," she said on a hiss. "Who's here?"

He tugged her into the shadows, his T-shirt and jeans making him seem normal while his dark hair slashed shadows across his face. "I'm not sure. But I heard noises out in the back alley."

Esther followed him through the house, the moonlight filtering through the windows guiding them. "I keep the gate to the alley locked. It's high and secure."

"Is it connected to your alarm system?"

"No. I only go out there once a week to leave the trash."

He stopped in the kitchen, away from the many windows. "Where is your actual studio?"

"Off my bedroom and the kitchen, along the back of the house. It started out as a garage, but now it's a sun porch and my studio." Too nervous to keep explaining, she pointed.

"Show me."

They headed back the way they'd come. But Esther could hear a great rustling near the garbage cans in the alley. "Why are they looking there?"

"Could be searching your trash for information."

"Maybe that's why they didn't destroy the shop. If they were looking for papers on the diamond—"

"They didn't destroy the shop because they wanted to find us first and take care of us. They'll go back there—after they make sure we won't stand in the way." He leaned close, his eyes glistening dark. "They'd question you first, Esther. Then—"

"Kill me," she finished. "I understand." She tugged at his shirt. "But I wouldn't put anything about the diamond in the trash. Even if I had information I wouldn't be that careless."

"Well, they might assume you'd throw out some notes or an old map or something to give them a clue."

"I don't keep business papers here."

"Do you have anything else here? Any reports, papers, diaries that belonged to your father?"

She thought about it for a minute, but she was a stickler for keeping the antiques business away from her retreat here. Her father's books and papers were locked in a small office in the upstairs apartment. Thankfully, those men hadn't had a chance to discover the apartment. But she wasn't going to tell

Cullen that, not until she felt she could truly trust him. "Nothing of my father's is here. Except the letters you brought."

She broke free, grabbing for the letters and the pouch.

"Hurry," he said, tugging her toward the sun porch.

"We can't go out there," she said. "Let me call the police."

"I don't trust the police," he retorted. "And *we're* not going out there. I am."

"Not without me!"

He turned, his frown cast in shadows. "Now is not the time to be difficult. You stay here with the letters. If I'm not back in five minutes, I'm either dead or on the chase. That means you need to get as far away from here as possible, do you understand?"

She understood how things worked in her world. "I'll call the police."

He shook his head. "We're talking millions of dollars here, Esther. We don't know how many people Hogan has on his payroll. You do know that even though he has a home in Europe and one in California, he also owns property outside New Orleans, right?"

"I've heard that, yes."

The man owned a huge plantation, complete with a big house and several outbuildings. She'd seen the spread in the *Times-Picayune* a few years ago.

"Well, that means he could bribe anyone, including an official. He's got that much money and clout."

The noise outside increased. As did Esther's anxiety.

They were hidden inside the big studio now and Esther once again found herself in the dark with Cullen Murphy. Her latest work, a rock and stone structure that resembled a sword or a cross, depending on the angle, shot up into the room with a domineering presence. She'd used the clock theme again and she'd even placed a few doorknobs in interesting shapes up and down the slanted angles.

Cullen glanced around, then lifted a heavy branch of polished wood. "Mind if I use this as a weapon?"

"No." She'd found the oak limb after the last storm, and sanded and polished it, but she'd hadn't decided how to use it yet. "Cullen, be careful."

"Turn off the alarm so I can get out. Then reset it, okay?"

"Okay."

She wanted to go with him, but she did see the logic of splitting up. So she waited until he was out the door and quickly reset the alarm, then rushed back to grab her clothes and purse. Tugging on jeans over her short nightshirt, she twisted a scarf around her neck, threw on a lightweight sweater and stuffed the letters into her tote bag. If he didn't come back, she could sneak out. If he did come back, they could still get away.

Or she could call the police, like a logical person.

Before she had time to decide, she heard a tapping on the French doors of the studio. The moonlight played tricks on her eyes. Squinting, Esther hid near a supply cabinet.

"It's me," Cullen called. "Let me in."

Esther hurried to hit the alarm. "Are you all right?"

"Yes." He pushed inside and watched her reset the alarm. "It was a very large dog, searching for a midnight snack."

"Elmo," she said, relieved but still shaking.

"Elmo?"

"The neighbors down the way have a Great Dane. He sometimes manages to get out of his dog run."

"Must be a very big dog run. He looked like a horse."

"He's a big baby, actually."

"Nearly gave me a heart attack," Cullen said, still watching the backyard. "I shooed him away, but honestly that is the biggest dog I've ever seen in me life."

Esther started giggling. "You're scared of Elmo?"

Cullen looked affronted. "I didn't say I was scared of a dog. I said he scared me. Especially when he lunged for me."

She laughed again. "And started licking your face? He's a friendly giant."

"You think that's funny, luv?" he asked, moving toward her.

She couldn't stop laughing. Whether from the adrenaline or the look on his face, she laughed until tears were running down her cheeks.

"He really was quite huge," Cullen said on a whine. But he kept advancing toward her with a smile.

Soon, Esther felt a table behind her and had to stop. But she kept on laughing. Then she looked into his eyes and saw something more, something that had nothing to do with dogs and thugs and giggling.

Cullen finally grinned, then reached out to push hair out of her eyes. "You're beautiful when you laugh."

Esther stopped to stare up at him, her heart caught against her throat. "I…uh…"

He tugged a hand through her hair, bringing her close, his smile soft and sure. Esther prepared herself for a kiss from an Irishman.

But she only got a peck on the cheek and a warning whisper in her ear. "We still have to be careful. I'm pretty sure that dog scared off the real intruder. I found footsteps all over the dirt driveway back there."

Esther stood watching the sun come up through the old, moss-covered live oaks that lined the property. Sometimes, she'd take her coffee and stroll through the intricate garden of Lara's amazing estate. The fact that her friend was a European princess who actually lived in a castle "across the pond" didn't impress Esther nearly as much as the fact that Lara had inherited this beautiful estate from her mother's side of the family. Esther thanked God every day for being able to live and work here. And she thanked God for such a friend as Lara. Lara was a gracious, down-to-earth woman who worked to help people in crisis all over the world.

Esther thought about her own quiet life and chided herself for not reaching out to others more. Maybe once this whole diamond affair was over...

Now, on her first chance in weeks to have a couple of days in her studio, she had a handsome Irishman for a houseguest and some nasty goons trying to torture her for information or outright kill her.

"Not exactly a quiet weekend," she mumbled as she whirled for more coffee. Knowing that someone had been snooping around recently put a dark cloud over this otherwise beautiful morning.

Esther closed her eyes and said a fast little prayer.

And opened them to find Cullen standing in the hallway, his hair wet from his shower, his clothes endearingly rumpled but clean.

"Coffee?" she asked, hoping he didn't hear the squeak in her early-morning voice.

"Yes, please."

"Did you get any sleep?"

"A little," he replied. "But I kept having nightmares about your friend Elmo."

She smiled at that. "He wouldn't hurt a fly."

Cullen advanced into the kitchen and took the coffee she offered him. "That sun porch settee gave me a sore neck."

He'd insisted on sleeping out in the studio, so he'd have the best vantage point of the whole backyard.

"I'm sorry you felt it necessary to do that, but it did make me feel better."

"All quiet so far," he said. Then he reached for a blueberry muffin. "Mmm, good. My mum makes blueberry muffins. My favorite."

"I like them, too," Esther said. She sat down to have one.

"I like to bake when I have downtime, but I can't eat it all so I freeze things. We won't starve."

He took another bite. "A woman of many talents."

"No, just someone who has a lot of time on her hands on the weekends."

She cringed, wishing she could take that back. But Cullen didn't give her a sympathetic look or stare at her as if she'd grown warts.

He laughed. "You, with time on your hands. You run an antiques store and you're an artist. I would imagine other women only wish they could be so together and organized. You might have noticed from your father's letters that he bragged on you a lot. You need to brag on yourself every now and then, don't you think?"

His thoughtful words touched Esther. "Thank you. That's awfully nice of you. I'm really nothing special."

"But you've had some success with your sculptures, right?"

"Yes. I've had a couple of great exhibits and I've been commissioned to create pieces for several well-known people. That's how I wound up living here. My friend who owns this place—she commissioned me to create a sculpture for the foyer of the main house."

"See, this mysterious friend trusts you. And knows good talent when she sees it."

"Again, thank you." Esther wasn't sure if he was being sincere or patronizing. Maybe he was trying to take her mind off everything else.

But someone had been prowling around out there last night.

She glanced over at Cullen. "How do you think they found us?"

"You'd be surprised how easy that is. They could have followed our taxi—the most logical way—but I checked and rechecked on that. Or they could have already known you have a home here. Or someone could have alerted them."

"So for all we know, they might have been watching me for a while now, too."

"Yes. Even before I showed up." He gave her a direct stare. "Did your father discuss the diamond with anyone else?"

Esther leaned against the counter. "He was discreet about such things. I don't recall him chatting it up with anybody. He told me some things time and again, but that was usually when we were alone—having dinner or unpacking things in the storeroom. And it was mostly speculation, and those moments were rare. He didn't like talking about it too much at work. I think he felt the same as me. He thought the diamond belonged in a museum."

She lifted up, the heat of Cullen's gaze hitting her. "Which makes me wonder why he wanted you involved. Did you tell him you intended to sell the diamond to the highest bidder?"

"No. We never discussed that."

"So you led him to believe—"

"I didn't lead him on, if that's what you're implying. After I got in touch with him, your father wanted me to come to America to discuss and explore several possible locations. We never discussed what would happen if we did find the diamond. He was willing to fund an exploratory expedition."

Esther didn't know what to say to that. "My father didn't have that kind of money."

Cullen looked down into his coffee cup. "He seemed to think he did, luv."

"Well, I didn't receive a big inheritance. What else was he hiding from me?"

"I don't think he was hiding anything so much. More like not divulging dangerous information. He didn't want to involve you, for obvious reasons, no doubt."

But Esther didn't see it that way. Jefferson Carlisle had been a shrewd businessman and a good father, but he'd also been moody and silent at times. Had he been thinking about that diamond and how it might change his life? Did he resent her because she was a burden that kept him from his dreams? She had to wonder what her father had told this man and what Cullen wasn't telling her.

"So what do we do now?" she asked, because she didn't know what else to say or do. Her father was dead and gone. But Cullen was very much alive and here. She had to find a way out of this mess so she could get back to her life.

Her boring, dull but safe life.

Cullen stared out at the backyard. "Whoever was out there will probably be back. We have a few hours of daylight to try to figure out if your father was on to something or if this is a wild goose chase."

Esther welcomed the busywork. It would keep her mind off her troubles and…off the man who'd come so close to kissing her last night.

"I need to see about the shop, too," she said. "Our customers will want to know what's going on, so I need to get with the locksmith right away."

"Then why don't you take care of that first."

She nodded. "I'll call the security company and then I'll see about a new front door. Ted can help with that. He said he'd put a sign on the temporary door, saying we were closed until further notice. Even though the police said they'd watch the shop, someone might try again."

"Very good assumption," Cullen replied. "If you need to go to the shop, I'm going with you."

She bristled at that. "So you've set yourself up as my protector?"

"Yes."

The one word was short and sweet and firm. No argument.

"Then I guess I'd better get used to having you around."

He winked at her. "Good idea."

Trying to get back to her sensible self, Esther cleared the dishes. "After I take care of the shop, we should sit down and go over my father's letters again. I noticed a pattern. He underlined certain words in each letter and even repeated those same words in other letters. There might be something there."

Cullen came around the counter and grabbed her hands. "You are so smart. I never noticed that and I should have. I thought it was a quirky habit to emphasize his excitement."

"Maybe you didn't read them with the same clarity," she replied. "After all, he was my father. I know his style. And if I know my father, the clues are written right there for us to find." She let out a little gasp. "He used to play games with me when I was little. He'd hide certain items around the shop and give me clues as to where to find them. A word here, an item there. But each word and item always led me to the surprise. And sometimes that surprise would be outside of the shop, sometimes we'd walk the whole city or even go to the zoo, until I found what I was looking for. Could this be the same?"

Cullen's eyes brightened. "Yes, certainly. He had to be careful, and maybe he was trying to give me hints, but he probably planned the letters so you'd eventually see the clues. He knew you'd recognize the game."

"I'll give it a try."

"If you're right, that means we're that much closer to finding that diamond."

"Possibly."

Cullen squeezed her hands and leaned close. "Your papa always said you'd figure things out."

Esther pulled away, his triumphant words jarring her. She'd already figured one thing out. He was using her to get to the diamond. But then, two could play at that game.

"So you need me to decipher the puzzle of this diamond, correct?"

He nodded, his expression full of what looked like relief. "Yes. We can work on it together."

"Yes, of course we can."

"Then you understand the importance of this?"

"Oh, yes. I do. And I hope you'll understand the importance of this diamond."

He lost some of his triumphant luster. "Meaning?"

She leaned in, a bit of glee in her words. "Meaning, I'll help you. I'll try to find a pattern in the coding of those letters. But only if you'll promise me something."

He leaned across the counter, staring her down. "What's that?"

"I want that diamond safe in a museum. Do you understand?"

Realization dawned blue-gray in his eyes. "We've already had this discussion. Now you're giving me an ultimatum?"

"Yes. It's that or nothing from me. And I'll be forced to go to the authorities if we can't strike up an agreement. Those are my terms."

He pushed a hand down his face. "You can't be serious."

"Do I look like I'm teasing?"

Cullen glared across at her. "Your father convinced me you were a sweet, accommodating woman."

"My father was a nice man with a kind heart, but he taught me to stand up for myself and to fight for the things I believe in. And I believe in saving beautiful, historical things such as a diamond that could have possibly been on a robe that belonged to one of the priests from the Twelve Tribes of Israel." She smiled and held out her hand. "I believe in that so much, I'm willing to risk everything to help you. Do we have a deal, Cullen?"

SEVEN

Cullen should have remembered the sensitive nature of women. After all, he had sisters. He'd often been caught in the middle of great dramas. His mother and his father had fought. His sisters and his mother had fought. His father and he had fought. Then they'd all fought. Manipulation and enabling had always been the rule of the day.

Probably the main reason he'd run shaking from any kind of emotional commitment. Entanglements were messy and stifling, the way watching his mum and sisters fuss and fight had always been. His father hadn't helped much. Once the fight was out of him, he'd go to work, silent and stoic, fulfilling his duty without a word to his son on how to handle the opposite sex.

Cullen didn't need that kind of drama. And he certainly didn't need the cool, calculated way Esther Carlisle had roped him and tied him to a post with her *terms*.

"I never lied to you about my intentions, Esther. Of course, I need you. I need your help. I only meant that your father always said you were clever. So maybe he did leave some clues for you to help me. But that doesn't mean we'll find the diamond."

"Don't even try to backpedal now," she retorted. "You've got me caught up in finding the diamond—and trying to save my life. If we work together, we can do that. But I need some sort of assurance from you that we can indeed work together. I mean, isn't that why you found it so important to return my father's letters? You obviously felt you couldn't do this without me."

He put a hand on his hip and stared down at the counter. "I'm here to find the diamond, darlin'. With or without *you*. It would be ever so much easier with you, however."

She mirrored his actions, her elbows bent and her hands on her hips. "Even though you know how I feel about this."

"I understand completely how you feel, yes."

He didn't understand the concept of finding something valuable then giving it up. Cullen lived for the thrill of the hunt, but he also liked being able to deposit large sums of cash into his bank account. Maybe he needed to explain how his family had oftentimes been hungry and cold and living from paycheck to paycheck. He worked his way through colleges and gone on wild expeditions to find valuable artifacts so he didn't have to feel that way again. And he surely didn't want his mother or his sisters to ever go without again.

Esther stood waiting, her tranquil patience irritating him. "I don't have to help you. But you have put me in danger and I did protect you from the police by withholding information. I've risked a lot for you, Cullen. Surely you can grant me this one favor."

So that was the way of it, Cullen thought. Feminine blackmail. Should he grovel? Or would good old-fashioned charm work better?

"Don't you wonder about the diamond?" he asked, hoping to touch her philanthropic heart. "Don't you want to find it a good home?"

She looked surprised, then indignant. "It's safe, wherever it is. Probably safer than it would be if you or those other treasure seekers got ahold of it. I want it to be salvaged, not scavenged."

"But you said it should be displayed."

"Yes, but I didn't say I wanted to pawn it off for money."

"A lot of money, luv. We could split it and you would have all the sculpture supplies you'd ever need. You could buy this estate right out from under your dear friend."

She wagged a finger in his face. "See, that's the difference between you and me. I wouldn't backstab a friend. But you would. So why should I trust you? You'll gladly walk right over me once we find that diamond."

He tried to keep a blank face. "You don't know me well enough to make that prediction."

"Don't I? You told me as much. You're a reformed criminal. You're in it for the money, for the fame, for the glory."

"And why are you here?" he asked, hoping to turn the tables. "If you're so concerned about me, you could have easily turned me in to the police."

"Because someone tried to kill me," she reminded him. "Because of you. You started this and you asked for my help. Now I'm in it up to my ears. Do we have to keep going over this?"

He frowned while she moved past him. "Okay, there is that, of course." He followed her to the sitting room. "Look, Esther, I'm sorry about all of this. But wouldn't you rather I get to that diamond before Charles Hogan and his henchmen? Because I can tell you right now, he'll use it for things you'd best not know about."

"What kind of things?"

"I don't have proof, but I've heard a lot of chatter about how he operates. He funds some very shady people. I should know, since I used to work for the man."

That little kernel of information caused her to turn pale. "And yet another revelation about your past. He's the criminal you worked for? And now he's chasing you because…"

"He is that man. The kind who chases people when they go against him. When I worked for him, I didn't realize how deep his retribution could run until it was too late. I paid for my sins, Esther. I had to do one last job then I got out from under him and I never looked back. But he's caught up with me after all these years and he wants retribution. He wants that diamond."

"So you're saying he might sell off the diamond and use the money for evil instead of good?"

"Exactly. He needs immediate cash flow and he doesn't want to leave a paper trail. Getting his hands on the Levi-Lafitte Diamond and selling it for a large sum of money would give him a lot of discretionary income." How could he make her see without revealing too much? "He does things that way. Buys up rare items and hoards them until he needs extra cash for his illegal activities." Cullen wanted to tell her he'd learned a lot from Charles Hogan, a lot about how to do things the wrong way.

"And what would *you* do with the money, Cullen?"

Thoughts of a nice, warm tropical beach came to mind. But when the image of Esther in a flowered, flowing, summery dress also came to mind, he had to rethink that daydream.

Instead, he went for hard reality. "I don't know. I know it's security, for my future, for my family. My mother is a hard-working woman, but she needs to rest."

That caused her to look at him in a new light. Those golden eyes shimmered with compassion…and regret. "I can understand that. But you'd get a nice finder's fee. You don't have to go after the whole enchilada."

"It's all or nothing with me, luv." In both business and pleasure, he admitted to himself. "Isn't that what you told me, too?"

She sent him a dainty little glare. "All or nothing, yes. But we still have a major problem. If I help you decipher those letters, you could also sell me to the highest bidder."

"What are you talking about?"

"You could get a lot of money from this Hogan man if you

tell him I have all the answers. How can I trust that you won't do that and make money on both ends?"

He chuckled. "Actually, that's a pretty good idea. If I were an idiot. Do you think I'd throw you to the wolves like that, really?"

"I don't know," she said, her tone prim and proper, her eyes deadly and dark. "You tell me."

"I told you," he said, coming around to grab her arm. "Esther, I couldn't do that to you, first because that's not right and second, because of the promise I made to your father."

"I can take care of myself," she said, pulling away. "You don't need to honor any promises. Except the one I'm hoping you'll give to me right now."

He slashed his hand through his hair. "I can't do what you're asking. Not with these people in the mix." Then he shrugged and let out a sigh. "But I will try my best to make sure the diamond finds a good, safe home—for a price. Since you asked so sweetly."

"I'm not asking, Cullen. If you want my help, then you need to reconsider my demands. I need a definite word of honor."

Cullen thought of his options—slim to none. He'd have to do as she asked, for now at least. "I don't have a whole lot of honor, but yes, I'll agree to your terms."

What other choice did he have?

"Thank you."

He brought her close with one hand on her arm and took his time studying her interesting face. "You're full of spunk, you know that?"

"Good. I'll need it, dealing with you."

"You'll need it to survive," he said on a low growl.

He wanted to kiss some sense into her, but that would be a foolish move. Then she'd probably go all gooey on him and things would get all touchy-feely. And confusing.

But he could see it there in her eyes, the question, the wonder, the hope. Was she attracted to him? How would she feel if she knew the truth about his past? That he'd done things for Hogan that went against everything he now believed? That he hadn't been completely honest with her at all?

Was he attracted to her? Every nerve in his body zinged a response while his brain tried to go off-circuit.

He'd made a promise he would surely have to break. It wouldn't be the first time.

"Let's get on with it," she said, her eyes changing from hopeful to resolute.

Cullen agreed, but suddenly wanted to get on with kissing her. And that realization made him jumpy.

"Okay, so I'll read over the rest of the letters and see what I can find," Esther said later. "Then, regardless of what you might think, I probably should go by the shop and help Ted take care of all the details of getting it back in order."

She had to do something to keep her sanity. Cullen was being agreeable, but she still didn't trust him past the front door. Ted had already called twice, worried about her. She couldn't keep putting him off, even though technically this was her first scheduled day away from the shop in a long time. Normally, Ted would have been able to handle things, but the robbery had left them jittery.

And her new partner in crime only added to the nervous lump inside her stomach.

"As long as I can go with you," Cullen replied. "And if you don't mind, I'd like to look around, too, since I never had the grand tour. I might be able to find other clues."

Great. Just what she needed, him poking around while she tried to stay focused. She thought about the upstairs apartment but still couldn't bring herself to mention searching there. She'd do that on her own time. "You think my father might have left information at the shop, too?"

"Stands to reason. If your theory on the letters is correct, then it would make sense that he'd do the same at the shop. You did say he used to play little games with you."

"Yes, but this is a bit more serious than a game."

"We have to think outside the box, Esther."

"And what if Hogan's men come back?"

"We'll deal with that when it happens. At least now we can be more alert on that matter."

"Are you even sure he sent those men? You said it might not have been him."

"No, I can't be sure. But I'm betting he did."

"But does anyone else know about your keen need to find the diamond?"

She watched as he turned thoughtful. The man really was nice-looking in a craggy, outdoorsy kind of way. He looked like a landscape waiting to be painted, or more like a solid piece of rock waiting to be carved into something beautiful.

But Esther didn't know if she had the strength to mold this man. He had stubborn etched in his jaw line.

"I don't know of anyone else who might be on my trail, no," he finally said. "I've learned over the course of my career to keep quiet when I'm on to something. Hazard of the trade."

"Then how did Hogan find out about this?"

Again, that evasive, secretive looking down at the floor. "That's the question. He has ways. His people are highly trained to listen in on conversations and tail people all over the world."

Esther turned at the bedroom door, her gaze scanning the room. "You don't think—"

"I've already checked. Nothing here." He shrugged. "But he could have easily bugged my apartment or my classroom."

"How did you get involved with Hogan in the first place?"

"He had lots of college students on his payroll, especially those of us interested in archaeology. He hired me during my sophomore year to help with a rather delicate excavation in Peru. We talked about a lot of things at the time. I was in awe of him and considered him a mentor."

"You talked to him about the Levi-Lafitte Diamond, even back then?"

"Not exactly. I read about the diamond years later and started silently doing some research and, as I said, that's how I came across your father. Nothing much happened for the last few years, except my correspondence with your father. But a few weeks ago, some of my papers went missing. I'm pretty sure Hogan had someone go through my files and scan my laptop." He shrugged. "Since then, he's been hot on my trail."

"Why haven't you done something about that?"

He chuckled, his grin a bit condescending. "Really? You can't exactly make a man like Charles Hogan go away. I don't have the money or the resources to make that happen. So I've learned to stay one step ahead of him."

"Really?" she mimicked. She was rewarded with a dark frown.

"I'll handle Hogan," he finally said. "Right now, however, I want to keep you safe."

Tired and cranky, Esther looked outside. "It's such a pretty day. I can't imagine anything sinister happening."

"Imagine it, luv. A rock this big brings out the worst in people."

Didn't she know that already? she thought, watching him.

But she didn't say anything. "I'll be in my studio, reading the letters. I seem to be able to work better in there."

Away from him. She had to keep moving away from him.

He looked up from his phone messages. "Okay. Stay alert. Even in broad daylight, you're still in danger."

"I'm well aware of that."

Taking the letters and her third cup of coffee with her, Esther went out and settled on a stool at one of her work benches. Longing to pick up one of her rasps and get to work on carving something, anything, she instead opened the next letter.

In this one, her father described how he imagined the diamond looked.

If it truly was on one of the garments from the Twelve Tribes of Israel, I can only see the jewel as being rather large. It would have looked very ornamental, like a medal of some sort, in order to fit in with the other jewels reputed to be on the robe. Rubies, sapphires and emeralds would have also been on the garment and all of the jewels would have been rectangular in style. But the chocolate would have stood out because of its rarity. While we don't have any proof that this diamond was on the robe, the myth prevails. Probably because some of the descendants of the Levi tribe still to this day deal in diamonds.

Did you know about the myth that had people believing that certain diamonds were buried in deep valleys surrounded by snakes? That would surely keep the locals away since the snakes would have been poisonous. On the other hand, literally, some people believed if one held a diamond in his hand while praying or making the sign of the cross, the rock would heal all wounds or illnesses. Some even ingested diamonds for health purposes. I don't recommend that. One has to be careful about what one ingests, don't you think?

Esther stopped reading, but the word *poison* kept coming back. What was her father trying to say?

It all seemed like riddles to her now. After a couple of hours of poring over each word, she looked up to find Cullen standing at the door, staring at her.

"What's wrong?" she asked after seeing his dark scowl.

"I might be wrong about Charles Hogan," he said, his tone indicating he was rarely wrong.

"Why? What did you find?"

He came into the room and touched his fingers on a small chisel. Then he glanced around, his eyes going wide. "You realize you have all sorts of weapons here, don't you? You could stab me with one of these wicked knives or hit me over the head with a mallet."

"Don't encourage me," she teased, but the serious look on his face brought her back to the problem at hand. "What did you find, Cullen?"

"Hogan is not in the United States. He's somewhere off the coast of Africa, sailing on his yacht."

"He'd better be careful. Modern-day pirates haunt those waters." Esther remembered something in her notes. "My father happened to mention South Africa. Something about diamonds being discovered long ago near the Orange River. Blood diamonds now, of course. He compared the Orange to the Mississippi—apparently they are both rather long."

"Charles Hogan doesn't mind getting blood on his hands," Cullen replied. "It might be a ploy to throw me off his scent, but he wouldn't send his men after me unless he was nearby to enjoy the hunt, so to speak. I can't verify if he truly is out of the country. No one can confirm anything. This makes things even more difficult."

Esther stood up to stretch, then draped her arms across the back of her chair. "I didn't think it could get worse. Then who else could be after us?"

"I don't know," Cullen admitted. "Maybe those men weren't even after me. They could have been trying to ambush you, however, and when they realized someone was with you and willing to fight, they made it look like a robbery of sorts."

"But they didn't take anything of value."

"Not yet," he said, his worried gaze moving over her. "Not yet, luv."

"Do you enjoy scaring me?" she asked, wishing he wouldn't look at her that way. That seemed much more dangerous to her right now than mean men chasing her. His gaze, those dark eyes moving over her like a soft, gentle rain, made her think of things she could never have, wish for things she'd long ago given up on. She needed to take her time and pray about all of this. Seek the Lord's guidance for her peace of mind.

"I'm not trying to frighten you, Esther. I want you to be on high alert. This is serious business."

Esther could see the serious all over his face, but she refused to be held captive in her own house. "Well, then, if we can't figure this out, I'm going back to my shop. I'm responsible, Cullen. I have to take care of this."

He advanced another foot or so. "I hope you don't mind that I'm here. I've thought about leaving, to draw Hogan away, if he's out there. But I'd feel better, staying close."

Esther wondered about the wisdom of allowing him to shadow her. He made her jumpy and off-balance and she needed all her wits about her if she wanted to find out what was really going on. But he might come in handy around the shop. The man did seem to have an eye for details. Maybe he could help her pinpoint anything off-kilter in her inventory.

As long as he didn't pinpoint anything off-kilter in her heart, of course.

"Since we're in this together, I don't see how you can leave. I fully expect you to live up to your end of this bargain."

He eyed her with a new understanding…and a new dare. "Are you holding me hostage, Miss Carlisle?"

"If you want to call it that, Mr. Murphy. But I'm only holding you to your part of our agreement. Because if you fail me, Charles Hogan won't be the only one chasing you."

He actually grinned at that. Then he moved toward her and leaned over her shoulder. "So you'd chase me around the world?"

She found her next breath and inhaled the spicy scent of

his aftershave. "To get what I want, yes. But you might not like it when I catch you."

He chuckled near her ear. "Don't tease me, Esther."

She whirled off her stool and stood to glare at him, her bark much worse than her bite. "I'm not teasing."

EIGHT

Esther introduced Cullen to Ted as a friend interested in purchasing some antiques and estate jewelry, although it was hard for her to swallow that particular description. She wasn't sure yet if the man was friend or foe, even though he had saved her from being harmed on two occasions now. After their discussion earlier, she'd found it hard to breathe, let alone think. He had a way of flirting while discussing anything. Even dangerous situations.

"I'm visiting New Orleans for a few days to do some research and maybe find a few treasures," Cullen explained to Ted, his words flowing as smoothly as cream into coffee. "I knew Esther's father. Wonderful man. And an expert on history and artifacts. I'm a history buff myself. I deal in a lot of artifacts."

"What kind of artifacts?" Ted asked, his Adam's apple bobbing. "Maybe I can be of some help."

"I hope so," Cullen continued, his hands held together behind his back as he strolled around the shop. "I like the clocks—fascinating. And I want a special piece of jewelry. I'll know it when I see it."

"He's one of those," Esther chimed in, hoping Ted couldn't see the nerves jumping right below the surface of her skin.

"We have a wide range of furniture and accessories. And of course, we have exquisite jewelry," Ted said, lifting his hand in the air. "Esther's daddy loved clocks and doorknobs. Esther, have you shown Cullen the doorknobs yet?"

"No," Esther replied, thinking this was awkward. "After what happened last night, I've barely had time to visit with him."

Ted's radar seemed to go up on that comment. "Were you here last night, Mr. Murphy?"

Cullen glanced at Esther. "I came in the shop right before closing. But this morning, Esther and I talked about what happened."

Well, at least that was the truth, Esther thought.

"I see," Ted retorted, hurt splotching his white face. "Esther, could I speak to you in the office?"

Esther shot Cullen a warning glance. "Excuse me."

Cullen nodded and went back to studying the cluttered offerings. He seemed more intent on finding that diamond than worrying about lying to her assistant.

Ted whirled as soon as they were out of earshot. "Why didn't you mention *him* as the customer you had last night?"

Esther didn't know how to explain without possibly putting Ted in jeopardy. Cullen had insisted they keep this between them. And maybe he was right. If the press got wind of a million-dollar diamond allegedly being hidden in the city or buried in the swamp, things could become crazy and dangerous.

"I was so distraught last night. What does it matter now?"

"He might have seen something," Ted said, dropping his hand against his side. "The police should talk to him. He might even be a suspect."

He might indeed. *Dear Lord, forgive me, guide me, please.*

"I didn't see the need to involve him."

She didn't like withholding information from Ted, but she was caught in an unfamiliar world, a nasty, secretive world. And she wanted to get out of it as soon as possible.

Ted paced the floor in front of her desk. "I am worried,

Esther. They only took a few inexpensive baubles. I think they were looking for something else."

"Such as?"

"I don't know. The safe is secure. The cash register is secure. Even the bank bag in the office safe is still there."

Esther came around the desk. "You're right. This whole event has been odd. I wasn't thinking straight last night. I'm going to do another, more thorough inventory. In case I missed anything. I'd appreciate your help."

"Absolutely," Ted said, bobbing his head. "Speaking of that, I'd better get ready for the repairmen. They should be here at ten. Do you think we should try to open?"

Esther looked at the boarded-up door. "It'd be better to wait until we hear from the repairmen. We didn't have any scheduled appointments today. If we open, we'll have to take all of that plywood down. We can't keep re-nailing that wood back on the doors. But we keep that sign up, explaining our temporary closure."

"Good idea. I'll check on the sign and I'll be glad to supervise the repairs." He glanced into the shop. "What about him?"

"What about him?" Esther retorted. "He wants to wander around. He promised he wouldn't be underfoot."

"All right," Ted said. "He's your friend, not mine."

Esther could have sworn she heard a bit of disapproval and warning in that declaration.

Cullen loved the smell of old things. The scent of softened leather mixed with the musky smell of aged books and the lemony scent of polished wood. He roamed around the shop, his gaze hitting on the shimmering chandeliers and tasteful table lamps, his fingers brushing over the faded brocade of a love seat or the worn brown of a leather high-backed chair. He tried to look casual while his mind whirled with possibilities. Clues to the diamond could be hidden anywhere inside this cavernous building. Lots of furniture with lots of drawers and cabinets and hiding places. Cullen opened a drawer here, loosened a door there. He looked high and low, but then who in his right mind would hide an exquisite diamond in plain sight?

While he searched and admired, he kept his eyes open for anything that might seem out of the ordinary, any type of clue that would lead him to the diamond. Esther might be on to something regarding her father's letters, but she hadn't finished putting anything together yet. In the meantime, Cullen decided he'd memorize each and every part of this vast collection.

The shop was tastefully done with "rooms" set up to display furniture and accessories. The old high-backed sofas and matching side chairs looked formal while the more modern pieces were displayed around colorful wool rugs and stunning hanging lights and chandeliers. The walls held expensive art from both local artists and well-known painters. Esther had placed a few of her own iron and stone sculptures here and there. He noticed she used the clock and doorknob motifs a lot in her work. He could see the whimsy of Esther in every corner. She might dress rather staid and steady, but the woman had an adventurous side.

Must have gotten that from her mother, Cullen thought as he wandered for the tenth time near what he had dubbed the cuckoo-clock wall. How many noisy clocks did one store need? He'd checked each and every one, but the diamond wasn't there. Cullen wished for open spaces and fresh air, and maybe Esther on his arm down at the Café du Monde.

Had Jefferson Carlisle really hidden the Levi-Lafitte Diamond here? Or had Esther's father duped both of them?

Usually, Cullen lived for the riddles and puzzles required from his line of work. He loved digging for clues, studying old bones and petrified pieces of buried time. But now, when he turned to find Esther bent over the counter, her reading glasses tipped on that cute nose, her hair haphazardly up in a tossed bun, he had to stop and inhale a breath.

He could stop running if he could see her this way at the end of each day. Shaking his head, Cullen reminded himself of all the reasons he needed to take the diamond and leave the girl. But then the girl looked up and right into his eyes and he had to wonder if his intent had changed, after all.

"Hey, are you all right?" She came around the counter to stare at him. "Cullen, did you find anything?"

He'd found something, all right. A true treasure.

"No, not yet." He moved toward her, the old ceiling fans swirling enough air to make some of the chandeliers dance like wind chimes as he walked by. He'd already checked the glass and crystals in those. No diamond hidden in the light fixtures. "You have a very eclectic collection here. I'm sure your customers and clients appreciate it."

She glanced around with a golden-eyed pride. "I changed things up a bit after Father died. He was a stickler for traditional items. Me, I'm more inclined to bring in things that toss out traditional notions. It puts a fresh face on antique items, I think."

Cullen could see that underneath all her prim and proper surface, Esther did indeed like to change things up a bit. He suddenly wanted to be the one to help her with that.

"Where's your right-hand man?" he asked on a subdued whisper.

"Ted? Out back with the repair team. We thought it best to repair the doors to the studio and the back door first. The alarm company will fix their part once the new front doors are in place."

"Good. You can get everything back in proper order."

"I hope so. I don't want to go through that again."

She pushed at her hair. "Maybe I should wait awhile before installing the new doors. We have no way of knowing if those people will be back."

Cullen wanted to reassure her, but he didn't have that right. "I can't predict that, luv. But I'd feel better if, while we're trying to figure this out, you reinstalled a good alarm system."

"Of course. I can't leave expensive antiques and estate items in such a vulnerable state."

Cullen wished he could do more. "I've looked in every corner and cranny, checked in cabinets and underneath cabinets. I can't imagine your father hiding anything here, but maybe he did leave clues I'm not seeing." He listened as the first of the clocks started the hourly chime. "Why did he like clocks so much?"

Esther smiled and waited for the clock to strike three; then she glanced back at Cullen. "He was fascinated with time. He hated to waste anything, including each and every minute of the day. He liked to stay busy, whether it was in cataloguing a new acquisition or reading about some intriguing trinket he had yet to collect."

She picked up what looked like a glass ornament. "As Ted mentioned, he also had a thing for old, pretty doorknobs. Or rather, my mother had a thing for them. According to my dad, she loved to hold up a doorknob and imagine where the door had taken people. He used to tell me how excited she'd get whenever she discovered a new doorknob. She wanted to know the history behind it. He kept on collecting them long after she died."

She stopped, shook her head. "She had this one special knob picked out for the door to my nursery. But my dad never got around to installing it. I used it in one of my sculptures." Shrugging, she said, "He sold that one right away. I always think of my mother and wonder if another woman somewhere is enjoying my artwork. I wish she could have seen my work."

"Tell me about her," Cullen said, tired of thinking about treasure and diamonds. "What was her name?"

"Marilyn," Esther replied. "They met at Tulane and fell

in love immediately. He'd planned to be a lawyer and she wanted to teach. But my dad's family had owned this shop for generations. My grandmother ran it. She died while they were in college, so my parents took over. He was the only Carlisle left to do the job. Dad loved history and because she loved him, my mom quit school and helped out. He finished his undergraduate studies but never went to law school." She stopped, looked at the ticking clocks. "They apparently loved working together. I'm sure he was devastated when she died and left him with a baby girl."

This time, Cullen didn't stop to think. He pulled her close and hugged her against him, the scent of her hair as sweet and enticing as honeysuckle. "I'm so sorry."

For a moment, she relaxed into his embrace. Then she lifted her head and stepped back, words rushing out of her mouth. "It's okay. I know my father sacrificed a lot for me. That's why I'd like to help you find that diamond. It was his secret quest, and I want to finish it for him." Then she shook her head. "But I don't want any profit from this, Cullen. I want to find it and put it somewhere safe. That's what my father would have done."

Cullen saw the plea in her eyes, saw the question hovering below the surface. Hating himself, he couldn't offer her that particular reassurance and he couldn't pretend. But he could tell her the truth.

"Esther, I—"

"Oh, there you are." Ted hurried up the aisle, a frown flattening his face. "I found something interesting out back. Can you come and take a look?"

"Of course," Esther replied, her disappointment and embarrassment tucked away with the strand of hair she pushed out of her face. "I'll be right there."

She turned and followed Ted toward the back of the shop. And left Cullen there with the soft swish of the swirling fans and the slinky melody of the chandeliers humming inside his head.

While those annoying clocks kept right on ticking.

Esther stared at the bullet holes all around the courtyard studio. "Where are the repair people?"

"They went to get some more parts."

She hadn't been out here since yesterday. The whole place was in shambles, pottery broken, old boards and tree branches scattered, and bullet holes in most of the planked walls.

Ted studied the damaged walls. "I think there were three shooters here, but the cops didn't catch that."

Esther started perspiring. She slid her gaze back around the four walls. "What do you mean?"

Ted ran a hand over the shattered wall near the ruined French doors. "Look. These bullet holes are different from the ones in the back. And if you were running away and got out the back door, why are there holes here near this door?" He turned, suspicion clear in his concerned frown. Before she could form an answer, he said, "Someone was shooting back, Esther. You don't carry a gun. So who was it?"

Esther inhaled a worried breath, then turned when she heard footsteps outside the open doors.

"It was me," Cullen said, his hands in his pockets, his eyes centered on Ted. "I was the one shooting back."

NINE

Esther glanced from Ted's shocked face to Cullen. Why had he confessed like that?

"I can explain everything," Esther said.

"No, let him explain," Ted replied, clearly confused.

Esther could see the anger and hurt on his face. She couldn't blame him. He had a right to know what was going on. "It's complicated," she began.

"Yes, it is," Cullen said. He strolled into the messy, ramshackle studio as if they were having a tea party at the Hotel Monteleone. "And you're right, Ted. I need to explain." He shrugged, then looked at Esther. "I came here to look for one thing and one thing only."

Ted put his skinny hands on his hips. "Oh, yeah? And what's that?"

"A diamond," Cullen replied, his smile soft and sure. "A very rare diamond that I tracked to this shop."

Ted didn't look convinced. "So you walked into Carlisle's yesterday and asked Esther to show you this diamond?"

"Yes, that's exactly what I did." Cullen advanced until he was beside Esther. "I got here before the intruders."

He seemed to be putting himself between her and any questions. Cullen appeared comfortable playing protector. Probably came with the job. He'd protect his treasures, no matter what.

But she wasn't one of his treasures.

"It's true," she said, glad to level with Ted. "I was about to close, but I did show Cullen the collections we have on display. He was leaving when he saw the two men coming up Royal. He warned me they might enter the shop."

"And they did," Cullen said. "I'm pretty sure they were looking for me."

"Because of this diamond?" Ted asked, his Adam's apple doing that bobbing thing.

"Yes," Cullen replied. "Apparently, they want the diamond, too. But I can't be sure about that. They might be after me for something else entirely."

"Oh, and why is that?" Ted asked.

"Yes, why is that?" Esther echoed, surprise igniting her distrust all over again. What else was he keeping from her?

Cullen had obviously decided on full disclosure. "Well, I did tell you I used to be a criminal. I stole things for Hogan."

"What kind of things?" Esther asked, her pulse hitting against her temple with a forceful throbbing.

"Jewels." He shot her a hard-edged glance. "But...I also told you I did one last favor for Hogan and then I walked away."

"A jewel thief?" Ted's brown eyes widened, making him look like an owl behind his bifocals. "Esther, do you hear the man? A jewel thief helped you escape from two intruders? Isn't that like Judas pointing the finger at someone else?"

"Ted!" Shocked, Esther steeled herself against any more surprises. "Cullen, you didn't mention that before. You only said you'd done some illegal work for Hogan. Was this back in Ireland or here in the States?"

"A little of both—he held the threat of harming my family over my head. But as I said, I paid for that in more ways than I care to divulge here."

"We'd like to know anyway," Ted said. He waited for Esther to agree with him.

Esther felt sick at her stomach. She'd trusted Cullen and he was still hiding secrets. For all she knew, he was in cahoots with this Hogan man. "I want my nice quiet life back, so you'd better explain everything."

Cullen leaned against the work table. "I worked for Hogan for about four years. Worked and went to college when he didn't have me gallivanting all over the world. I was studying archaeology and art history, so he played on my keen interest in artifacts and treasures and offered me a full-ride scholarship if I'd help him out. I thought I was doing something good, finding the items on his list. I thought he actually admired my smarts and determination. But I never dreamed he was using his money to run an illegal arms empire. And he fuels that empire with diamonds, lots of diamonds."

"You can't be serious."

He gave Esther another direct stare, but she saw the plea in his eyes. "I found out the hard way that Hogan was a not only a crook, but an international criminal of the worst sort. It made me sick. So I offered him a trade-off, something he wanted, to let me go. It was risky, but I offered him a way out for both of us."

Esther sure knew that risky feeling. Listening to Cullen tell the story made her think of dark shadows and daring deeds. *He's not a hero,* she reminded herself.

Cullen glanced over at Ted, then back at her. "I didn't have much of a choice. I wanted to finish college and I needed to support and protect my family." He looked at Esther, his eyes holding hers. "My father was an alcoholic. He died when I was in high school and I fell in with a rough gang. I didn't care that my mum had to raise the three of us. But when I matured I realized my sisters deserved better and so did my mother. Interpol and the CIA both wanted to nail Hogan. They caught me, hoping to reel in a bigger fish—Hogan. In exchange for my help, they promised to clear my record. This was a chance to regain some of my dignity." He looked down at his feet. "They arrested some of Hogan's underlings based on my information, but his slick lawyers protected him. They could never prove anything so he went free."

"But you're free and clear now, too?" Esther asked, hoping he did have noble aspirations instead of criminal intent. He'd been through a lot, but she refused to allow her empathy to overrule her sensibilities.

Cullen nodded, his gaze still on her. "Yes. Free and clear as far as the international authorities are concerned. I still do the occasional covert job for them here and there. I have lots of connections."

She understood what he was telling her now. He could protect her and he could override the local authorities if need be. "But Hogan never forgave you?"

"He never knew I was the informer. I left his organization after I delivered a particularly exclusive package to him. I offered him something he couldn't refuse. In return, I promised to keep my mouth shut."

"What was the package?" Ted asked, completely caught up in the story now.

Cullen reached a hand toward Esther, letting it trail across her tools and trinkets. "A diamond."

Esther put a hand to her throat. "The chocolate diamond?"

He nodded. "Or at least, Hogan believed it was the Levi-Lafitte Diamond. He was too paranoid to let anyone appraise it, but I told him I'd had it appraised. Even showed him the paperwork—fake, of course. Hogan believed me, then he locked it away." He stopped, scrubbed his hand down his jaw. "All these years, he believed he had the Levi-Lafitte Diamond. But he actually has another diamond, a flawed yellow diamond. It's not worth nearly as much as the Levi-Lafitte. Which is why I have to find the real one. I don't want him to get his hands on it."

Esther understood now. "And now he's found out he doesn't

have the real diamond. He thinks you have it." She gasped. "Or he thinks my father had it?"

"Yes, and he's fighting mad because of his connections with Louisiana. He wanted to own a diamond found here, so he could show it off. Or sell it for profit. He keeps his illegal funding separate from his other businesses. Last year, he tried to sell the diamond he had and realized he'd been duped."

Ted jumped as if he'd been bitten. "Esther, the Levi-Lafitte Diamond? Did you know this already?"

She broke away from the ocean-deep pull of Cullen's eyes and nodded toward Ted. "Yes. Cullen thinks my father knew where the diamond was hidden. *The real one.*" She glared at Cullen. "And Hogan is after us."

Ted gave Cullen a hopeful stare. "You think Mr. Carlisle located the stone and he was holding out on you?"

"No, I think Esther's father had the diamond," Cullen replied. "Hogan knows I tricked him and now he's after the real diamond. Esther's father and I are the only real experts on its history. I have years of correspondence from Esther's father. I partnered with him after I went back to Ireland, hoping he could help. I believe Jefferson found it or knew where it might be. But he passed away before we could confer on any of it. I came here hoping Esther would know more. I have to find the real diamond before Hogan does. Or Esther could be in danger."

"She is in danger," Ted blurted, his fists tight against his khaki pants. "She should have told the police about you."

Esther whirled to hit a hand on the table. "And now that you've told Ted, he could become a target, too."

Cullen turned her around. "We're all in trouble. I refuse to leave New Orleans until I have that diamond. Hogan won't stop at shooting up your shop. He needs that diamond for funding, so he'll send more people, better-trained people, to finish the job. I tricked him. Now he wants to make a point."

"Or else?" she asked, anger making her brave.

"Or else," he replied, fear for her centered in his eyes.

Ted looked around. "Good thing you still have that gun."

Cullen wasn't worried about Ted. He only hoped Esther would understand his predicament. "I always carry a gun. I had the SIG-Sauer already and I bought the Remington from your friend Mr. Reynolds because I'm a collector. And because it gave me an excuse to case his shop before I came to you."

Esther stood tall, as she often did when she was angry, he noted. "So you came here knowing Hogan's men might follow you, tried to get me to hand over this diamond and then planned to talk me into splitting the profit with you—all before Hogan found out?"

He gave her a brief smile. "Yes, something like that. But I did have a weapon with me. I thought this would be an in-and-out job. But things turned way too complicated. Now we're in the thick of it."

"Yes, we certainly are." She went to the door to stare at the three bullet holes in the wall. "Your aim seems to be off."

Aggravated by her dismissal, he said, "But you were very close with that pretty pottery you threw."

Esther looked embarrassed, then explained to Ted, "I had to wield the Remington, but I used pottery and tools to distract our intruders while Cullen shot back at them."

"A shoot-out, Esther." Ted went even paler than usual. "You could have been killed. And you didn't tell the police any of this."

"I didn't have time," she said, shaking her head. "Cullen warned me not to trust anyone."

Ted tugged at his thatch of hair. "I guess that included me and the Reynoldses. We were all so worried about you."

"Cullen was working to get us to safety," Esther said, clearly contrite because she'd been less than honest with Ted.

"I can see that," Ted said, pointing to the bullet holes everywhere. "I'm surprised Mr. Indiana Interpol Murphy here didn't kill one of them, at least."

Cullen frowned. "Well, I was holding a blow torch in one hand and the gun in the other. But the SIG-Sauer is one of the best. It made for good cover so Esther could get to the door. And—I was dodging bullets, too."

Ted gave Cullen a doubtful look followed by a twisted grin. "Well, I'm impressed. I'd love to hear more about your adventures, Mr. Murphy." Then he stomped toward Esther. "But you need to get these people out of our lives. Esther doesn't deserve this. Over a diamond, of all things."

Cullen understood the young man's anger. Esther looked ready to do murder. He needed to calm both of them. "I'm sure I'll have an opportunity to do that, since I intend to stick around for a while."

Esther started out the door. "We need to go over the shop, search for any clues again, maybe papers or interesting features that might be hiding that diamond. I want to find it and get it out of my life." She shot a frown back over her shoulder. "It's caused me nothing but trouble."

Cullen shot Ted a covert look. "She's a hard taskmaster."

"Don't I know it," Ted replied. "But she means it."

Cullen could see that Ted was smitten with his boss. Not that the kid was that much younger than Cullen. But he'd need all the help he could get in trying to protect Esther. Maybe Ted would find something to help with their quest.

"So you were close to Jefferson?" he asked as they locked down the studio and headed back to the shop.

Ted shot him a hostile glance. "I was raised by my aunt and she died when I was a teenager. Mr. Carlisle pretty much took care of me from then on out."

Cullen had to tread lightly. "I guess you and Esther are like sister and brother then?"

Ted sent a quick glance toward Esther. "We're close. We've only got each other now."

That didn't really answer the question that screamed inside Cullen's brain. How close? He'd watched the two of them together and it seemed Ted had a definite crush on Esther. But not so much the other way around. She didn't seem to notice, or maybe she had noticed and tolerated the affection.

Cullen wasn't sure why this should bother him so much. It was none of his concern if Esther and Ted had a thing. But he didn't like it, nonetheless. Not at all.

Not that it mattered one bit. Esther didn't save any smiles for Cullen. She only glared at him and frowned behind her adorable bifocals.

Right now, she was going through shelves and opening old books only to shove them back in place. He feared if he approached her, she'd throw a heavy tome at him.

"Esther," he called.

She kept right on working the far corner of the showroom.

Walking fast to get to her, he stopped short of grabbing her close. "Esther, that's it. What I told you and Ted. That's the truth." But not all of it.

She whirled like a pretty top and yanked off her reading glasses. "How can I even begin to believe that? You think my sickly bookish father masterminded a diamond dig and actually found it?"

He picked up an old tarnished doorknob with painted flowers on its porcelain center. "I haven't given you any reason to trust me. I didn't want to hide my past from you, but it was an ugly past and I'd rather keep it buried. It's too hard to explain, too hard for people to understand."

She blinked, then refocused. Her lashes were so thick and long they looked like woven silk. Did she wear a special kind of makeup to get them that way?

"Cullen, you can't bury things away all the time. You're in the business of digging things up, of finding lost discoveries, of tearing through other people's personal things with a certain disregard. So why is it so hard for you to open up about your own life? You know a lot about me, knew it before you ever walked in the door. But I don't know that much about you."

She dropped her glasses onto the receipts by the cash register. "I'm beginning to think I'll never really know you."

"He's only been here two days," Ted, his new worst enemy, stated from a safe distance. "It's impossible to know someone in that short a time."

Esther glared at them. "Ted, make sure those repairmen get the job done before the end of the day. I'll call the salvage yard and find out if they can deliver the new front doors tomorrow. The sooner we get back to normal around here, the better."

She dialed the number and gave the command, her tone crisp and no-nonsense, her adorable, accusing eyes centered on Cullen.

Cullen took "getting back to normal" to mean she wanted no part of him. Well, he couldn't leave her alone and in danger. And he couldn't leave here without that diamond. But he couldn't tell her the rest of the story, either.

"Have you had a chance to work on those letters anymore?" he asked, hoping to distract her.

Wrong assumption.

Slapping at the phone book, she asked, "Is that all you think about?"

She huffed past him so fast, a display of scarves and hats seemed to dance as she went by.

"No, that is not all I think about," he replied, his own anger hitting the surface. "I'm concerned about you. I want this over so I can get back to my own life, too."

"Good."

"Good."

She marched into the office and started clearing away papers. "I have to get this organized, if you'll excuse me." She started reading over each sheet, her eyes moving at breakneck speed. "As for the letters, I'll get back to them tonight when we get home—" She quit in midsentence. "When *I* get back home. You should either stay in a hotel, or go home with Ted. He might know more about that infernal diamond than me. He used to encourage my father to go for it."

Interesting, Cullen thought. But right now, he had other things to consider. "Did you bring the letters with you today?"

"No," she said. "I hid them in a hat box in the back of my closet."

"Esther?"

"What?"

"I wish you hadn't done that."

She pushed some trade books back onto the shelf behind her desk. "Why?" Then she stopped to stare at him. "You don't think…?"

Cullen felt it in his gut. The letters might hold the key to finding the diamond. But if someone else got to them first, it would be disastrous. "We'd better get back to the Garden District, right now."

She grabbed her purse and her cell phone, terror battling with anger in her eyes. "We'll take my car."

"Hey, where are y'all going?" Ted called.

"Be back in a few minutes," Esther shouted. "Once the repairs are done, don't open the doors to anybody else."

TEN

They made good time getting to the carriage house, but Esther's heart was racing to catch up when they exited the car. She'd driven well above the speed limit.

"I hope we're not too late," Cullen said as they rushed toward the back door.

But the door was standing open.

Esther slammed against him. He reached for her, instinctively putting her behind him. "They might still be here."

"The alarm was supposed to go off," she said.

"Yes, but that's not a guarantee. I told you they could easily disarm an alarm. And you weren't here to hear anything."

"What should we do?"

Cullen pulled his travel pouch around, then took out his gun. "We go and investigate."

Esther wasn't sure she wanted to investigate, but anger at being yet again violated made her push forward. "Go, then."

Cullen held the gun with both hands. "Hold on to me."

She grabbed his shirt, glad for the lifeline. What had she been thinking, hiding the letters here? She should have taken them with her. Now they might be lost forever. The clues and her father's precious words.

They made it into the kitchen only to find the whole room ransacked. Kitchen drawers were tossed to the floor, the pantry door stood open, cereal and rice dumped from their containers. Cookies lay scattered here and there amid granola bars and Esther's stash of dark chocolate.

Obviously someone thought she'd hidden the diamond in her food supply.

The living area wasn't much better. Pillows overturned and slashed, knickknacks broken and destroyed. Thankfully most of this stuff belonged to her and not Lara.

"We'd better check the other rooms," Cullen whispered. They went toward the guest room, but when they heard a crash in her bedroom, he whirled in that direction. "Stay here," he told Esther.

"No, I'm going with you." She was right on his heels before he could protest. "I want to see who's in there."

"I don't think it's your friend Elmo the giant dog this time," he said over his shoulder. "Stay behind me and duck down."

She crouched, the memory of bullets whizzing past her during yesterday's shoot-out still fresh in her mind. How had her life turned into such a nightmare?

Cullen crouched in front of her, then with his gun held in both hands, jumped into the bedroom. "Stop right there!"

But the intruder didn't stop. He took off running through the open studio doors then hurried through the French doors out of the studio. Cullen raced after him, firing a shot.

Esther watched as the big man, dressed in street clothes, kept right on running across the yard. He was wearing a navy sock cap and dark shades so it was hard to tell if he was one of the same men who'd attacked them yesterday. At least this one didn't have a gun.

Cullen sprinted across the yard and out the fence, but Esther heard a car motor revving. She took off in the direction Cullen had gone, praying he wouldn't get shot.

She heard gunshots when she got closer to the fence, followed by tires screeching. The loud grinding of gears indicated the culprit had gotten away.

Then silence.

Her pulse beat loudly against her temple. She reached the open gate, out of breath and scared that something had happened to Cullen.

Closing her eyes, she prayed he'd be okay. "Cullen?"

No answer.

Down the way, a dog barked. Probably Elmo, wondering what the ruckus was about. "Cullen, are you there?"

Birds sang high up in the live oaks. Palmetto palms waved in the slight breeze. "Cullen, please answer me?"

Esther glanced around. It was late afternoon on a lazy summer day. This alley was usually quiet during the week, but this was the weekend. Surely someone was at home. What if her neighbors had seen this and called the police?

Where was Cullen?

Bracing herself, Esther swallowed and started through the open gate, her prayers centered on finding him alive. With one quick move, she pushed herself into the alley, her gaze searching the sandy lane and high fences.

Then she saw Cullen lying in the middle of the worn path. And he wasn't moving.

"Cullen." Esther rushed to him, then bent down to listen for any signs of life. He was breathing.

Letting out a sigh of relief, she glanced around. No one was outside, no one seemed to be watching. Then she moved her hands over him to make sure he wasn't wounded. She touched his head and felt blood in the tufts of dark hair near his temple. Someone had whacked him across his skull.

"Cullen, can you hear me? Wake up!"

He moaned, grabbed at her hand.

"You need to wake up," she said, still holding him.

He opened an eye and stared up at her. "I think I've gone to heaven. I see an angel before me."

Slapping at his arm, she sat back on the ground. "You scared me to death."

He groaned then held his head while he struggled to get up. "I'm sorry." Then he came fully awake. "I think he got away."

"I can see that." She pushed off the ground, then offered him her hand. "Let's get you inside."

He reached up for her hand, but when he tried to stand, he turned pale and fell back down. And brought her tumbling with him.

"Hello," he said, a lopsided grin coloring his face in spite of the pale hue of his skin. "My angel is here to rescue me."

"You could have been killed," Esther said to hide the little thrills moving up and down her spine. They'd hugged briefly earlier, but she'd never been *this* close to him before. In spite of his injury, he looked dark and dangerous and very much alive. "We...we need to get back inside."

"Yes," he said, dragging the word out. "Too dangerous for you out here."

She untangled herself and tried again. "Can you sit up?"

"Yes." He pushed with both hands. "Give me a minute."

Esther searched the area again, glad they were partially hidden by the fence and shrubbery. "Did he shoot at you?"

"No, but he came running toward me like a bull. And then his friend in the getaway car started shooting." He winced as he managed to get up on his knees. "The big one tried to knock my gun out of my hand. I got in a shot, but it missed him. Then he knocked me back against the fence. I think I hit a steel post or something. I don't remember much after that."

"You might have a concussion," she said as she put her arm across his back. "Can you stand now?"

He used the fence as leverage, then made it to his feet. "I'm up, luv. Good to go. Do you see my gun?"

"No. I guess they took it."

"Great. They can use that against me. Plant it in a not-so-good spot. Frame me."

"Don't worry about that right now," Esther said. "Hold steady to me."

But he wobbled like a top.

"You need a doctor."

"No doctors. Just get me inside."

"Why do you shy away from normal people?"

He leaned on her as they slowly made their way back to the house. "I have you. Don't need normal."

"But I am normal," she replied, her eyes touching on his too-close face, his too-bright eyes. The man had beautiful eyes.

"Not you're not, not really."

"You have a point. Normal people wouldn't go searching for a diamond that probably doesn't exist. Normal people would call the police and an ambulance and tell the truth. I guess I'm not so smart after all."

He grinned and grunted. "You're okay in my book, luv."

Ignoring the little shivers of awareness moving through her system, she helped him through the doors to the studio, then dropped him onto an old chaise lounge. "Let me go find my first-aid kit."

"Esther," he called, a hand up, "go look for the letters first. If he found them, we're in trouble."

She nodded and hurried to her bedroom. It had been searched, too. The bed pillows were on the floor and her armoire stood open. Esther ran to the closet. The door was open. Her heart nearly stopping, she looked inside. Some of her clothes had been rearranged and tossed but the hat box where she'd hidden the letters was still in the same spot.

Esther bent and lifted the lid, then moved away the scarves and wool hats. The letter pouch was still there. They'd made it in time. *Thank You, Lord.*

Letting out a relieved breath, she held on to the pouch and stopped by the bathroom to find antiseptic and bandages.

"Good news," she said when she came back into the studio. "I found the letters." Cullen wasn't in the lounge chair.

"Cullen?"

"Over here."

She turned to find him standing by a lampshade, one hand on the rim. "What are you doing?"

He held a finger to his lips. "Bugs," he mouthed. He stopped, then grinned when he pulled out a tiny black speck that looked like a pea. "But not anymore."

"They bugged my studio?" Esther dropped her supplies and the pouch.

"Probably your bedroom and the kitchen, too," he replied, his voice low. "I'll check the whole house."

"You need doctoring."

"I'm fine. Just a bit dizzy."

"Cullen?"

"Esther?"

"Okay, go look for…those contraptions. I'll be right behind you."

She grabbed her stuff and followed him. "That means they heard us talking last night."

He nodded. "Yes, so they know about the letters now."

"And that's why they came back today," she whispered.

He put his finger back to his lips, then leaned in close. "Don't say anything more until I check."

Esther pursed her lips and started cleaning away debris. Mad that someone would invade her home and do this, she was very aware that this situation was fast getting out of hand.

While Cullen took it slow and ran his fingers over every lampshade and picture frame, Esther cleared the kitchen, made some coffee and called the shop from her cell to tell Ted what was going on.

Ted didn't answer his cell, so she left a message. "We're okay. Just clearing up some things." She didn't dare say what things. She only hoped Ted would figure it out. "Call me and let me know you got this message. Go ahead and close up and go home. I'll check with you later."

She made scrambled eggs and toast and waited for Cullen to finish. By the time he'd made it back to the kitchen, he looked beat.

"I didn't find anything else," he said. "I think our visitor came in yesterday to plant the bug. That's why we saw footprints by the fence. He probably jammed your alarm system long enough to get in and out. Then they listened in last night and decided to hit again today, while we were away."

"They must be watching my apartment and the shop," Esther said. "I don't like that idea." She shivered in spite of the warm day. "I need this to end, Cullen."

He sank down on a bar stool. "I'll make sure of that. If we can figure out your father's clues, we can find the diamond and…I'll be out of your hair."

With the diamond, she thought.

"Let me check your head, and then we'll eat."

He didn't argue with her. Esther cleaned the wound, carefully washing it with antiseptic.

"Ouch, that burns."

"Sorry. You have an abrasion, but it's not a deep cut. When's the last time you had a tetanus shot?"

"About a year ago. I'm all caught up on shots."

She found a big bandage and dressed the wound. "Are you dizzy? Seeing double?"

He turned and surprised her by catching her hand in midair. "No, Nurse Esther. Two of you would be nice, but I'm fine. I'd had worse bumps from riding a camel."

Esther's whole system hummed from his touch. And from the way he sat there, looking at her. "You've ridden a camel?"

"Many times. You should try it."

"I'm not a big adventurer like you."

"Yes, you are. I think you'd love to go on a grand adventure."

"You think that about me?"

"Yes."

She pulled her hand away and cleaned up. "Well, I say let's get out of this predicament and then we'll see about that."

He took both her hands in his this time. "Esther, I will get you out of this. We'll finish cleaning up this mess, eat our food and then we'll sit down together and decipher those letters."

Esther felt his eyes on her. She looked over at him, her gaze hitting his, her hands clutching tightly to his fingers. For that moment, she believed he'd live up to that promise. For just that moment, she saw something there in his vivid eyes.

She saw a longing, a need, a hope.

He leaned in, his gaze moving over her face. "You know something? I'd like very much to kiss you right now. How would you feel about that?"

She couldn't move, couldn't think. How *would* she feel about that? "We've only known each other two days, Cullen. Actually more like twenty-four hours. And in that time, my shop and my home have both been vandalized, we've been shot at, I've told little fibs to everyone to protect you and someone tried to steal my father's letters. I don't know if I should kiss you just yet."

He tugged her close. "It would make me feel a whole lot better." He touched a hand to her face. "Or it might make me even dizzier than getting hit on the head."

Then without a word, he held her chin in his hand and leaned in to touch his lips to hers. It was a soft, searching kiss, sweet in its intensity and very sure in its strength.

Esther fell into his embrace, her brain screaming warnings while her heart sang with joy. She thought she heard bells ringing.

She did. But it was her cell phone.

Pulling away, she gave Cullen a wide-eyed look. "Excuse me." Breathless and shaken, she said, "Hello."

"Esther, it's Ted. I need help. We've been hit again and this time, they found the safe."

ELEVEN

"What was in the safe?" Cullen asked after they hurried to the shop.

"Some very exclusive coins and toy soldiers, some rare books," Esther replied on a winded breath. "And some jewelry."

"Jewelry." So Miss Golden Eyes had a few secrets of her own. "Anything I might be interested in?"

"No," she said on an aggravated note. "The diamond is not in my shop. I wish I could put an ad in the paper stating that."

"But you failed to mention you had jewelry in a safe."

"Yes, I failed to mention that. Just like you failed to mention a lot of things." She burst through the back door, calling out Ted's name.

Cullen hurried ahead of her. Didn't she realize she might be in danger, barreling in the back door like that?

"Ted, where are you?" she called again.

They heard a weak whimper. "In here."

"The storage room," Esther shouted, running toward a door down a small hallway. A door he'd never noticed before. Come to think of it, he didn't remember this hallway, either.

Cullen hurried to keep up. "Be careful. It might be a trap."

Esther didn't seem to hear. She ran through the open door into the dark storage area. Cullen followed, praying Esther wouldn't be taken by Hogan's men.

"Ted!"

"I'm down here."

Esther sank down to where Ted was hiding with a phone clutched to his chest. "Are you all right?"

Ted bobbed his head. "They knocked me down and I twisted my ankle. By the time I got back here, they'd busted open the safe and left."

Cullen saw the gaping door. "This is at least two inches of solid steel. How'd they get in?"

"We have a code," Esther said, glancing up. "They'd have to know the numbers."

"I gave them the combination," Ted said on a whine. "They threated to torch the place, then go after Esther."

"I'm surprised they left without hurting you more," Cullen said. It wasn't like Charles Hogan to leave a live witness. He checked Ted for any other injuries and saw a rising bruise and a nasty cut on his left cheek.

"They hit me and knocked me down." Ted held up the phone. "I had this with me since I was away from the desk. It rang while they were going through the safe. One of them knocked me down and they ran out. I think the phone scared them. I'm sorry, Esther. But they said they'd find you next."

"You did the right thing by cooperating," Esther said. "Let me help you up."

"Did you call the police?" Cullen asked. Covering his hand with an old rag he found on a table, he felt around in the square safe. Nothing. "They took whatever you had in here."

Ted looked at Esther. "I didn't know what to do. I called you first. Should we let the police know?"

"We have to," Esther replied. "Those items were insured. We have to file a report."

She helped Ted onto a nearby packing crate. "I'll call right now." The look she gave Cullen dared him to protest.

Cullen listened as she gave the 911 operator the report. This was getting messier and messier. Frustrated, he remembered thinking this would be a clean job. In and out, if he'd had his way. But things were not going his way.

And the more he lingered, the more he put Esther in danger.

He turned to Ted. "Did you recognize the intruders?"

"No," Ted said. "They were wearing dark hats and sunglasses. But I bet it was the same ones who hit us yesterday. I guess they came back for one more try."

Which meant they wouldn't quit until they had what they wanted. "Very bold, considering the police know about the first break-in."

"They didn't seem too worried about being bold," Ted replied. "They had big guns and…they were big men. I had to protect the shop and Esther."

"Of course you did," Cullen said, trying to reassure the agitated young man. Whoever these people were, they obviously thought Esther had that diamond. He was amazed they'd let Ted live.

She came back to stand with him. "Ted, let's get you in the office, where it's cooler. Cullen, will you help me?"

Cullen lifted Ted up. "Can you stand?"

Ted tried his right ankle, then winced. "I can hobble, I reckon."

"Hold on to me then." Cullen helped him so they could slowly make their way across the shop and into the office. He looked around at the open file cabinets and papers all over the floor. "They had a second look in here, too."

Esther waited for the patrol car. "I've had enough. We have to stop this. One at my apartment and two more here. Our list of culprits is growing."

Cullen agreed. "You need to shut down the shop and get a twenty-four-hour guard. They'll be back. It's too dangerous."

"This is my work," she retorted. "How can I just shut things down?"

FREE Merchandise is 'in the Cards' for you!

Dear Reader,

We're giving away FREE MERCHANDISE!

Seriously, we'd like to reward you for reading this novel by giving you **FREE MERCHANDISE** worth over $20. And no purchase is necessary!

You see the Jack of Hearts sticker above? Paste that sticker in the box on the Free Merchandise Voucher inside. Return the Voucher promptly...and we'll send you valuable Free Merchandise!

Thanks again for reading one of our novels—and enjoy your Free Merchandise with our compliments!

Pam Powers

Pam Powers

P.S. Look inside to see what Free Merchandise is **"in the cards"** for you!

LIS-FM-12B

We'd like to send you two free books to introduce you to the Love Inspired® Suspense series. These books are worth over $10, but they are yours to keep absolutely FREE! We'll even send you 2 wonderful surprise gifts. You can't lose!

REMEMBER: Your Free Merchandise, consisting of **2 Free Books** and **2 Free Gifts**, is worth over $20.00! No purchase is necessary, so please send for your Free Merchandise today.

Plus TWO FREE GIFTS!
We'll also send you two wonderful FREE GIFTS (worth about $10), in addition to your 2 Free Love Inspired® Suspense books!

YOUR FREE MERCHANDISE INCLUDES...

2 FREE Love Inspired® Suspense Books

AND 2 FREE Mystery Gifts

FREE MERCHANDISE VOUCHER

**2 FREE
BOOKS
and
2 FREE
GIFTS**

Please send my Free Merchandise, consisting of
2 Free Books and **2 Free Mystery Gifts**.
I understand that I am under no obligation to buy
anything, as explained on the back of this card.

❏ I prefer the regular-print edition   ❏ I prefer the larger-print edition
    123/323 IDL FS5T   110/310 IDL FS5T

Please Print

FIRST NAME

LAST NAME

ADDRESS

APT.#   CITY

STATE/PROV.   ZIP/POSTAL CODE

NO PURCHASE NECESSARY!

▲ Detach card and mail today. No stamp needed. ▲

© 2012 HARLEQUIN ENTERPRISES LIMITED. ® and ™ are trademarks owned and used by the trademark owner and/or its licensee. Printed in the U.S.A.

LIS-FM-12B

The Reader Service - Here's how it works:

▲ If offer card is missing write to: The Reader Service, P.O. Box 1867, Buffalo, NY 14240-1867 or visit www.ReaderService.com ▲

BUSINESS REPLY MAIL
FIRST-CLASS MAIL   PERMIT NO. 717   BUFFALO, NY

POSTAGE WILL BE PAID BY ADDRESSEE

THE READER SERVICE
PO BOX 1867
BUFFALO NY 14240-9952

NO POSTAGE
NECESSARY
IF MAILED
IN THE
UNITED STATES

Cullen didn't have time to answer. They heard the sirens outside. Then Cullen heard a woman's shrill voice.

"Esther? Ted? Are y'all all right in there?"

"It's Mrs. Reynolds," Esther said. "Cullen, will you explain to her?"

Cullen went to the back door, thinking for such a secluded entryway, this one had a lot of traffic. "Hello," he said, holding the door so the perplexed woman couldn't enter.

"Who are you?" she asked, her expression guarded.

"I'm a friend of Esther's. We've had a bit of a problem, but we're okay now."

"I want to see Esther," the woman said, her tone insistent. "I hear sirens."

Cullen felt a hand on his arm. Esther pushed past him. "Hi, Mrs. Reynolds. We're okay. But we've had another break-in."

"Oh, my." The gray-haired woman put a hand to her heart and pursed her bright red lips. "Someone is surely pestering you. The devil's always in the details."

"Yes, I'm afraid so," Esther replied. "But we're okay. I have to let the police in to investigate."

The woman clearly didn't want to leave. "Where's Ted?"

"He's inside. He's fine," Esther said. "I'm sorry, but I have to direct the officers." She pointed behind Mrs. Reynolds to where two uniformed officers were coming into the courtyard, guns at the ready. "Over here," Esther called.

Cullen waved Mrs. Reynolds away but felt the brunt of the woman's disdain hitting him like little daggers.

"After I talk to the police, we have to come up with a plan," Esther said to him. "I won't live in fear, Cullen."

Cullen didn't want her to live in fear.

He wanted her to be safe again.

Even if it meant giving up his quest for the diamond.

"One week."

Esther gave Cullen her second ultimatum in as many days,

then waited, her hands on her hips. They were back at the carriage-house apartment now and it was late into the night. While she still got the shivers thinking about people lurking about and breaking in, this was her home. She wouldn't let these buffoons scare her away.

The police went over the shop for prints, but based on Ted's statement, the men had been wearing gloves. And no one had noticed them slinking through the back way and into the courtyard. Ted claimed he'd been so busy unpacking inventory in the storeroom that he hadn't even heard them coming through the open back door.

This was New Orleans after all. People in the Quarter tended to live and let live. They'd probably thought two delivery men had arrived. That was what Ted had believed until they'd pulled out guns. But they'd been delivering something far more dangerous than anyone expected.

"I can wrap this up in a few days," Cullen replied. "I thought I'd covered my tracks, Esther. But obviously, Hogan has spies everywhere. I'm beginning to think someone who attended one of my lectures must have alerted him to my whereabouts."

"Did you discuss this trip with anyone?"

He shook his head. "No. I tend to keep my travels to myself because of this very thing. Hazard of the trade. But I think if we put our heads together, we can solve this and I'll be on my way. You'll be safe again."

She wished she had his confidence and his seemingly blasé attitude about doing the job then leaving. "I can't afford to wait any longer," she said. "I usually take a one-week vacation at the end of summer. We close the shop down then. I'll take an earlier vacation this year, I suppose." She sat down at the dining table, her father's letters in front of her. "Let's get busy then."

"Will Ted be okay?" Cullen asked. He took a chair across from her, his eyes on her instead of the letters.

In spite of everything, Cullen seemed truly concerned. As well he should be. She tried to ignore his dark, searching eyes or the look of remorse on his face. She tried to forget how he'd kissed her earlier, too.

"I had Mr. Reynolds put him on a bus to his sister's house in Baton Rouge. He can rest and take care of his sprained ankle and that cut on his eye. He's traumatized by all of this."

Cullen scowled. "He seemed that way, yes."

Esther saw his scowl as a sarcastic one. "Are you making fun of my friend, Cullen?"

"No. Just making an observation." He leaned forward. "I'm glad you were with *me* when this happened."

Esther stood up so fast, letters spilled onto the chair and floor. "Ted could have been killed. That's why I decided to shut down for a week. I can't risk that again." She wrapped her arms across her midsection. "This will hit the papers soon and that won't help our reputation. I've already had calls from the surrounding shops, asking what's going on. This could ruin Carlisle Collectibles."

Cullen got up and took her by the arm. His touch reminded her again of their kiss…and her guilt at what had happened. She wanted to pull away, but his gaze held her there.

"Esther, I'm sorry. I blame myself for all of this. But if we work together, maybe we can figure this out and stop the attacks. Please?"

She refused to let his nearness or that pull from his incredible eyes draw her in. Sending up a prayer for self-control, she said, "I said a week, Cullen. That's all I can give."

"I understand." He tugged her close. "I'm here and we're going to figure this out." He let her go to reach down and pick up the letters that had scattered on the floor. "We start here, with the letters, okay?"

Esther's willed her heart rate to settle. But she insisted on calling to check on Ted first. "He should have made it to Baton Rouge by now."

A little while later, she put down her phone and turned to Cullen. "Ted is safe in Baton Rouge. He promised he'd go to a doctor there tomorrow and get his ankle checked."

She was safe here for now, she reminded herself. Cullen had secured the place, checking doors and windows, setting traps here and there to alert them of any intruders. At least the man had some unconventional ways of protecting her, probably due to being out in the field with few resources and little protection.

He'd checked all the hedges to make sure no one could hide in those. He'd put a stronger lock on the back fence and a trip wire across the back patio in case anyone made it that far again. He'd fixed the motion lights, setting them to go off if anything bigger than a bug moved in the yard.

Small measures, but Esther felt safe again. For now.

"Okay," she said, willing herself to the task ahead. They had a bowl of popcorn and some fruit and cheese to nibble while they read through the letters. "I'm ready." She took a sip of her iced tea, then studied another letter. This one had been written a year before her father's death.

Dear Cullen:
Did I mention that in ancient times, meat was thrown into the diamond pits so that _falcons_ would go down and eat the meat and possibly _ingest_ a diamond or two in the process? Not sure how the humans found the _falcons_ or even found the diamonds _inside_ the birds' stomachs but that's one of the myths I've studied since I began my fascination with diamonds. Maybe they _poisoned_ the birds so they'd die right there or just outside the pit.

"There's that word *ingested* again," Cullen said, making a note. "I can't believe I never picked up on that or the word *poison* before."

"You were reading these letters to hear about diamonds, not birds or poison."

He gave her a thoughtful glance but didn't say anything.

Esther read another earlier letter, amazed and touched that her father had recalled how he used to take her to the Audubon Zoo when she was small. Those precious memories seemed overshadowed by danger now. How she wished she could have one more day with her father.

When Esther was a little girl, she had this <u>white</u> play dress. She'd found it in the shop in a box of old clothes and insisted she had to have it. I guess because it looked like a <u>wedding</u> dress. She'd put it on with some of her mother's old shoes and she'd march around, calling herself a princess. I found an old tiara and put it on her head. What a beautiful sight. One day right after that, I took her to the zoo and she spotted the <u>white tigers</u>. She squealed and said those were her tigers because they matched her princess dress. <u>Zulu and Rex</u>—those were their names. I believe they are still at the zoo.

"I remember that, too," she said out loud, causing Cullen to glance up. "He used to take me to the zoo. I hadn't thought about that in years. I loved the birds and the tigers. I think I have a book of Audubon prints he bought me for my birthday. It's reproductions, of course, and not very valuable, but it's around here somewhere."

She smiled over at Cullen, almost letting the memory fade away. Then her head came up. "Maybe I should find that book. We need to check every resource, right?"

Cullen nodded. "Anything he underlined, we'd need to verify in some way. He's obviously sending both of us some sort of hidden messages."

Esther hurried to the long bookcase lining one wall of the

den. "I have so many books here, but I'm sure I still have that one. I'd never give away a book my father gave me."

She moved her fingers over the shelves, then grabbed her notepad to study some of the words she'd written down. "So far, I have swallows and poison, stolen, ingested, folklore and now falcons and these others—white, Zulu and Rex. You were right. He mentions the word ingest or ingested and underlines it several times."

Cullen jotted down some more notes. "So the workers ingested diamonds to smuggle them, and the birds inadvertently swallowed diamonds to bring them out of the mines. Maybe the swallows aren't birds at all, but another form of ingesting? What does that have to do with poison, though? And what does that have to do with finding the Levi-Lafitte Diamond?"

"The workers thought the diamonds were poisonous," Esther said, her hand landing on a thin book. "I think I've found it!"

She pulled the book out and let out a triumphant yelp. "This is it. Let's have a look."

Cullen came and sank down on the sofa beside her, the scent of his earthy aftershave merging with her own floral perfume. Esther focused on the aged book, willing herself to ignore the man sitting there with her.

"Look for a falcon," he suggested, his eyes on the Audubon sketches and artwork. "Beautiful renditions, aren't they?"

Esther nodded. "Audubon is one of my favorites. One of the first sculptures I did was based on a blue heron he'd drawn. The sculpture was rather badly done, but my father loved it. He kept it on a windowsill upstairs."

Cullen smiled at her. "You've said your father didn't talk much, but it seems he always had time for you. That's a blessing, isn't it?"

She nodded, then held a hand to the book. "Yes. I'd forgotten how hard he tried with me. He was a private, quiet man, but I know he loved me. And he taught me what faith is all about—to never turn from God's love."

She stared at a rendering of a blue heron. "Blue, blue?" Dropping the book, she looked down at her notes. "I remember something blue in one of the letters. I wrote it down." She scanned the notepad. "Here! The Blue Hope Diamond. He'd underlined that several times in one of the letters. Do you remember discussing it?"

Cullen nodded. "Yes, he mentioned how the Hope diamond was considered to be cursed since most of the people who owned it died young or went into poverty. And of course, we know what happened to King Louis XVI and Marie Antoinette. They once owned that diamond."

Esther shuddered, remembering her father's written word. "Yes, but he said in spite of all that history, it wound up here in the States, in Washington, where a wealthy socialite owned it and wore it as a necklace."

Cullen put his fingers together, then rested them on his chin. "Cursed, lost, found again, and all over three centuries or more. It's not the same size in carat weight, but what else would it have in common with the Levi-Lafitte Diamond?"

Esther thought back over the history of both diamonds. "Well, one theory has the Hope Diamond originating from the eye of an idol. And we know that the Levi-Lafitte Diamond supposedly came from a robe that belonged to one of the priests from the Twelve Tribes of Israel. That's something in common, at least."

"But is the chocolate diamond cursed, too?"

He looked so serious. "I don't know. But I'm having a lot of bad luck myself right now. Besides, I don't believe in such tales. I have faith that we'll figure this out."

"Faith," they both said at the same time.

"Hope," Esther said. "Faith, hope…love?" She let out a gasp. "He quoted that passage of Scripture from First Corinthians, Chapter 13, in one of the letters and he underlined those three words. He was talking about the power of diamonds and the path to true love. 'So faith, hope and love abide, these three; but the greatest of these is love.'"

"Is that the message?" Cullen asked, his gaze washing over her, a tenderness flowing through his gray-blue eyes.

Esther's heart beat so loudly, she was sure he had to hear it. "That's a mighty stretch, don't you think? I do have faith that this will be solved, but beyond that I'm not sure what will happen next."

Cullen leaned closer, his smile full of hope, at least.

"As for right now, though—"

Esther couldn't breathe. The man had a devastating smile. It pushed away everything bad and shined brightly on everything good.

He leaned close and whispered in her ear. "I think I know what will happen next with us."

Then he pulled her into his arms and kissed her.

And all of Esther notes fell in a pile at her feet.

TWELVE

Esther lost track of time. Not even a ticking clock could pull her away from Cullen's kiss. She was caught in a haze of sweet longing, a cloud of total security and trust. Here in the midst of discussions about diamonds and birds and intrigue and danger, she felt completely safe and secure for the first time in a long time.

Then he drew back to stare down at her and the spell was broken. Her flush washed hot over her face and neck. "I…"

He touched a finger to her lips. "Don't. Don't tell me you're sorry. Because I'm not."

Esther gulped a breath. "I don't know what to say, what to feel. You're…you're you and I'm—"

"Beautiful," he said, his hand touching on her face. "Beautiful." He pulled at the clasp holding her hair up, dropped the intricate comb on the table with a clatter and tugged her back into his embrace.

Esther's hair was suddenly down around her face and shoulders. His fingers moved through it, combing it, curling it. He held her head with his hands. His lips came back to hers, and she accepted him and reveled in how much she enjoyed being in his arms.

Was this wrong? Or was this part of that faith, hope and love the Bible and her father talked about? Could she have those three things with this man? Her father had taught her about the importance of love, about the importance of putting God and her family first. Only now, she didn't have a real family.

And Cullen Murphy wasn't the type to settle down and produce a family. Her doubts nagged at her like water lapping at a shore, taking bits and pieces of her back out to sea.

She managed to pull away. "We have to be careful, Cullen."

"I know. I'll protect you from these people, no matter what."

"No, I mean careful about…this. *This* is dangerous, too."

"Extremely, but I kind of like it," he said with a wolfish grin. Then he feathered little kisses down her cheek. "I enjoy kissing you."

"I…I uh…enjoy it, too, but…we have to be aware."

He fingered a stray curl. "I'm very aware of you, luv."

Esther stood and pushed at her hair. What kept bothering her, holding her back? Something, besides the reality of this wild adventure. Something. "You're a big distraction. We have to get back on track, remember? Figure out the clues, where the diamond might be?"

"I'm on track." He sat there, his gaze moving over her in a way that had nothing to do with diamonds. "I'm right where I want to be."

Esther wasn't used to giving in to such temptations. "I can't…allow this…until we stop these people. I can't let you get to me this way. My whole life has changed in a matter of hours. I need to think this through."

He got up, stalked her like a big lion. "Do I get to you?"

"You know you do," she said, wanting to be angry. But the thrill of *him* kept her from lashing out. "You do, Cullen."

He had her back in his arms, his hands crushing her hair again. "You get to me, too. Maybe your father was on to something besides a fifty-carat diamond."

She held her arms against his chest. "Or maybe he was trying to warn me. About you."

Cullen stepped back. "I saw nothing like that in those letters. The man adored you, talked about you a lot in our correspondence. I feel like I know you because of that. I wanted to come here, meet you, protect you." He stopped, stared down at her. "That's not exactly true. I wanted to meet you, but I never thought I'd want to…stay here and get to know you better. Or that I'd have to shield you from Hogan's goons."

"Exactly. I don't know you," she replied, steeling herself against his change of heart. "He never once mentioned you to me. And I haven't seen your letters to him. Why not?"

"I don't know. Maybe because he wasn't so keen on you knowing about his quest for the diamond or how that involved me. Maybe he never thought we'd become friends—that it would never come to this."

There it was again. The sense that he wasn't telling her everything. "Or maybe he was afraid it would come to this." She walked over to the empty fireplace. "Maybe he wanted you to find the diamond, but not involve me. The clues could have been for your eyes only, until the two of you could get together. But he died before that could happen. All that about faith, hope and love, or any comments regarding me, could be us speculating too much."

"Or it could be right on target." Cullen followed her. "Esther, you've never seen my replies, but there is one thing in them you should know. I promised your father that if anything happened to him, I'd be sure to watch after you."

"I don't recall seeing him ask that in any of the letters."

He looked down. "He didn't have to. I offered it."

Was he telling her the truth? He seemed so evasive at times. "And yet it took you a while to get here."

"I had to be sure," he replied. "I had a lot at stake."

She figured he had a definite lack of commitment at stake. "You want the diamond, Cullen. Not me. I'm just a means to an end."

He lifted his chin. "Why can't I have both? What's so

wrong with wanting to get to know you and also finding the diamond? It would mean security for both of us."

She only needed the security of his touch. But he obviously needed more. "Are you serious? You know how I feel, where I stand. I'll fight you on this. You not only made a promise to my father. Remember, you made a promise to me. If you intend to break that promise, I will make sure you regret it. You should know enough about me to at least know that."

He backed away, clearly shocked that his kisses hadn't won her over. "Maybe we should get back to finding clues."

"Good idea."

She needed to remember why this man was here. Remember what truly was at stake. He wanted the diamond. She had her heart to protect. Even though he'd agreed to her terms, he'd break that agreement out of greed and a need to win. He'd get the diamond and her heart, and Esther would be left with…nothing.

They couldn't have it both ways. And she couldn't allow him into her heart if he was the kind of ruthless man who'd take the jewels and run.

With the shop closed down, and with a handsome, kissable man sleeping in her den, Esther felt restless and unable to sleep. So instead of going to bed, she sat in the chaise lounge in a corner of her bedroom and continued to read her father's letters.

"Somewhere in here, there has to be an explanation," she said. She had to find it.

She went back over the facts. Her father thought the Levi-Lafitte Diamond did exist and that it could be hidden somewhere in Louisiana, possibly in or near New Orleans. Cullen had searched for the diamond for Charles Hogan but, having not found it, had replaced it with another one. He still wanted to find the real one and he thought her father might be able to help.

Due to their ongoing correspondence, Cullen had suspected her father might actually know the location, or that he'd found the diamond before he died. But Cullen couldn't decipher the underlined words in his letters without her help so he'd come here to see if she knew anything and to see if she could figure out what her father was trying to say. And so far, she couldn't make any sense of things.

Esther thought about Cullen's words to her earlier. He'd responded to her father's letters. Where were the letters he'd written? Having Cullen's responses would help clarify so many things—about the diamond and about the man.

She sat up, wondering why she hadn't thought of this before. What if the people who'd twice robbed her antiques shop had been looking for Cullen's letters to her father? If they knew enough to come to the shop, they might know about the correspondence between the two men, too. And they might think they could somehow find the answers there.

She got up to confront Cullen even if it was six o'clock in the morning. But then she thought about how he'd kissed her earlier, how that kiss had made her feel. Out of control but also out of breath. Secure but shaky. Cherished but tormented, too. Even after that, he'd hinted that he still wanted to sell the diamond for profit. She couldn't fall for a man who didn't share her same principles. Cullen would take the diamond and leave, happy to profit from his big find.

While she'd be left wishing she could kiss him again.

Esther sank back on the chaise. She could see the yard out beyond the windows across the back of the studio room. The security light was on, its yellow glow casting shadows through the towering live oaks and ancient magnolia trees. She used to feel safe here in her little hideaway. Now those shadows shifted and blurred, tricking her and taunting her. Someone could be out there watching her every move.

Would she ever feel safe again?

Only when she was in Cullen's arms.

No, she thought. *I can't depend on him for my security.* Cullen was a nomad, always on the move, always searching for that next quest. Esther had never given her heart to any man. She'd dated in college but nothing serious. And after her father died, she'd been too busy trying to keep his shop open and running to worry about affairs of the heart.

But then, she'd never dreamed a handsome adventurer would come into her life and steal her heart. Cullen had disrupted her world and shifted her way of thinking, but she wouldn't let him lay claim to her soul.

He would try, but he couldn't change her mind about what to do with the diamond. If she could find that diamond before Cullen did, she could get it to safety before he took it and left her.

But she'd have to betray him in order to do that.

Esther sat quiet and still, centering her prayers on doing the right thing. She knew what she had to do, but it wouldn't be easy. If there was such a thing as a fifty-carat chocolate diamond, she had to find it before anyone else did—to save it.

Would Cullen ever forgive her?

Did that matter?

She closed her eyes and prayed for strength and calm. She needed answers, maybe more than she needed to find the diamond.

Esther pulled out her cell and called Ted.

"Hello?" He sounded sleepy.

"Ted, I'm sorry to wake you, but I need your help."

"I'm awake. Name it."

"You have access to a computer, don't you?"

"Yes. I brought my laptop and my sister has Wi-Fi."

"Good. I need you to do some research for me."

Ted readily agreed. Esther told him about her father's letters and gave him the possible clues she'd received so far.

"I still have several letters to read through, but I need you to do research on these things and see how they could be connected. Or how they might each be significant when put together. They might all add up to a location or a place where the diamond could be hidden."

"I'll get right on it," Ted said, excitement crackling in his voice. "Esther, are you all right? That Murphy guy isn't badgering you, is he?"

"No. He's trying to help me get to the bottom of this. The police have assured me they're putting extra patrols on Royal Street to calm the other merchants."

"Good idea. I didn't like leaving, but with this bum ankle, I couldn't have worked anyway."

"You need to rest up," Esther said. "But you can help me a lot by doing the research."

"Good. It'll give me something to do while I'm sitting with my foot propped up."

She explained about the letters and gave him the list of prominent words she'd found so far.

"And one more thing," Esther said. "Do you know where my father might have stashed any other letters? Maybe some from Cullen?"

The line went quiet and then Ted replied, "If he kept any correspondence, it's probably in the upstairs apartment over the shop. Try the back bedroom he used as his office. You know, the one I've been trying to get you to clean out for months now. Since you won't let me do it, now's your time."

"Yes, I'm well aware of that messy office." Esther had avoided going through her father's papers and she refused to let Ted go into the apartment. She had the only key and she left the door locked so she wouldn't have to think about it. Maybe now would be a good time to do that very thing.

"Be careful," Ted said.

"Thanks." Esther hung up and sat staring at the letters in her lap. She hadn't been up to the apartment in days. The hidden door had been locked tight after each of the break-ins and she hadn't forced the issue with the police. She hadn't brought up the apartment with Cullen, either.

Had she? She couldn't remember and she wasn't very good at covert espionage.

The hallway leading up to the apartment was blocked by several boxes and a mock wall that really was a door. Most people never even knew about the upstairs apartment. It was a private pied-à-terre after all.

And Cullen hadn't discovered it yet. Esther wanted to keep it that way. She'd have to find a way to get back to the shop without him so she could go into that upstairs office and search for the letters he'd sent to her father.

Cullen couldn't sleep. He'd rather be in the studio, so he could have a better view of the backyard. But Esther had refused that suggestion. She didn't want him near her, obviously. The closeness they'd shared earlier had scared her away.

So here he sat in an armchair by the window in the long den, his eyes bleary and his mind racing. While he kept one eye on the backyard, he went back over all the conversations and correspondence he'd had with Jefferson Carlisle. Cullen and Esther's father hadn't always written letters to each other. They'd had several phone conversations, too. Those had been secretive and cryptic, but Cullen thought he knew enough to put the clues from the letters together with the suggested locations Jefferson had called him about. That was, until he'd let Esther read the letters and string together those catch phrases. Cullen had concentrated on the overall correspondence, not each individual word.

Cullen hadn't told Esther about her father's sporadic phone calls. Or that each call had become more and more desperate.

He knew he should tell Esther about that last phone call, but he'd been waiting to see if she suspected anything regarding her father's death.

Apparently she believed Jefferson had died from natural

causes—a heart attack. But Cullen had a notion that something has caused that heart attack. Something or someone.

Because Jefferson had known where the diamond had been hidden. But he'd been afraid to tell even Cullen, unless he saw him in person. So he kept writing cryptic letters instead, letters that Cullen couldn't decipher.

"Somewhere in the swamps near the bay, Cullen. You'll need to find certain markers, if time and the tides haven't changed the location. That last big hurricane changed the landscape but you should be able to find the landmark." Then Jefferson had made one of his odd requests. "Esther will remember things. If anything happens to me, find Esther. She can lead you to the diamond."

Cullen had waited for the next call.

It never came.

He couldn't bring himself to tell Esther that he believed her father's death hadn't been natural at all. He'd hoped to disprove that theory before he had to share it with her because that would mean he was responsible. He'd gotten her father involved in this. Now he'd gotten her involved, too. Maybe this diamond was cursed.

He believed Jefferson Carlisle had either been murdered or scared to death. If he could put together all the information he needed to find the location and the diamond, he could at least spare Esther that awful realization.

The next step was to arrange the clues into something that would help them find the exact location. Because there were a lot of swamps around here and all kinds of dangers in each of them. As the old cliché said, like looking for a needle in a haystack. Or one rare diamond buried in mud and cypress roots. And it had all started when he'd given Charles Hogan another diamond. Now that move was coming back to haunt him.

Cullen thought about Esther's fierce need to protect the diamond and his fierce need to protect her. If Charles Hogan was behind this, there would be no stopping him. But what if it wasn't his old nemesis?

What if someone else was on to this, too?

That thought chilled Cullen to his bones. He'd have to rethink everything. He needed to know if Charles Hogan was truly on his trail. And if not, then who else wanted that diamond?

THIRTEEN

Cullen came up off the sofa, wide-awake.

He'd heard a noise. Grabbing for any weapon, he spotted a long hollow bowl. At least he could hit someone over the head with the thing.

But after tiptoeing around the apartment with the bowl, he didn't see any signs of forced entry. He headed to Esther's room, his heart leaping ahead of him. Glancing in the door, he saw the tip of her head burrowed underneath the cover.

"Esther?"

No answer. She was sound asleep.

But he was once again wide-awake. Something had niggled at his consciousness all night long, something he wasn't putting together. Walking around the kitchen, he checked doors and windows, watched for moving shadows and tried to remember what was bothering him.

Thinking about Esther staying here alone gave him the creeps, but she had mentioned something about the apartment over the shop. Maybe she should stay there.

The apartment above the shop! That was the thing that he'd missed. He'd been going over and over the shop and this place in his mind, trying to figure out what he'd been missing—items that shouted clues, words or comments that told him he'd overlooked something important.

Esther had mentioned offhandedly the day they were attacked that her father lived over the shop, and then said so again here in this very room. What had she said? Something about one of her sculptures.

"The sculpture was rather badly done, but my father loved it. He kept it on the windowsill upstairs."

He must have dozed off right after he got that memory embedded in his brain. They needed to look in that other apartment.

He glanced at his watch. Six-thirty in the morning on a Sunday. This was too important to wait.

With a grunt, Cullen rounded the corner and hurried back into Esther's room. He hated to wake her. Maybe he should explore the apartment by himself. But then he'd have to leave her here alone.

He went to the bed to nudge her awake. "Esther?"

The lump on the bed didn't move.

"Esther, wake up."

He tugged at her head and came up with only a dark scarf. Cullen pulled back the covers and discovered…nothing. No Esther. And the connecting bathroom was empty, too.

Esther was gone.

Early morning in the Quarter was always pleasant, but a Sunday morning was even better. No drunken rowdiness, no loud music, no sirens wailing. Just the empty streets and the early tourists hoping to get a prime spot at the Café du Monde.

Esther was glad she'd taken the streetcar to get back to the shop. No one would notice if she sneaked into the shop at this early hour. A lot of her neighboring merchant friends liked to work in the quiet of a Sunday morning. And with no vehicle parked here, she could get into the apartment, search for any letters or other documents then take her bike back to the Garden District before tourist traffic even hit. She longed to go to church and sit in peace so she could pray earnest prayers for safety and well-being. But what if those men followed her to church? She'd put everyone in danger. Shivering, she rounded a corner and made sure she hadn't been followed.

She was safe, so far. She hadn't had a minute's peace since this had happened. Since Cullen had come into her life. She could use some alone time.

Unless, of course, Cullen woke up and followed her.

She was gone. Cullen kept telling himself that over and over again. But her car was parked outside underneath the little carport in the same spot where they'd left it last night.

No signs of anyone coming in. The doors were all locked up tight, windows secure. The big security light shined like a new moon on the backyard. Dawn was cresting, but he couldn't see any movement outside.

Had someone enticed her away with a phone call?

Or come in and held her, maybe even knocked her out?

Should he go after her or call the police and report her missing? If Hogan's men had Esther…

Cullen went back into her room. With intuition that had been honed over years of looking for hidden artifacts, he studied the long, tidy room. The bedcovers had been carefully fluffed to make it look like she was still there. The bathroom held the hint of her perfume, but there were no wet towels or washcloths anywhere. The closet was closed. He opened it, noted the clothes all neat and lined up by color, the many shoes done in much the same way.

Except the shoes she'd been wearing earlier weren't there.

Cullen remembered her long, floral skirt and pretty lacy blouse. The shoes—some sort of dark brown leather, part sandal and part Mary Jane. With a cork wedge!

He searched among the boots and flip-flops, the loafers and pumps. Good thing he had sisters, or he wouldn't have been able to identify what Esther had worn on her feet.

Except that he always seemed to notice everything about

Esther. And he distinctly remembered her kicking off those cute little shoes when she'd entered the house yesterday.

If she'd been surprised, she wouldn't have had time to put on her shoes. Unless the intruder had been polite enough to allow her to do so.

"Where are you, Esther?"

He searched the whole house from top to bottom and then started on the grounds. She was nowhere to be found.

But he did find footprints out behind the back gate. Tiny little, dainty footprints. And only one set.

Esther had obviously walked away.

Cullen tried her cell and got her voice mail. "This is Esther, proud owner of Carlisle Collectibles. Please leave me a message."

"Where are you?"

There. That was his message. Worry warred with aggravation while Cullen mulled over his options. Had someone taken her right from under his nose?

No, no way. He'd set up booby traps, made sure they'd hear lots of noise if anyone tried to enter the house. He went out into the studio and saw that one of his over-the-door trip wires had been disengaged.

Esther had watched him set that trap.

He had to do something.

Logic said she'd gone off on her own, something dangerous and unwise. He decided he'd take the car and head to the shop. If it had been burglarized again, Esther might be there. Then he had a thought.

What if Esther had decided now would be a good time to examine the contents of that upstairs apartment everyone had so conveniently forgotten?

Or what if someone else had taken her there with a purpose?

Esther could either be playing him, or she could be in

danger. Either way, he had to start at the shop and hope he found her before it was too late.

Esther opened the padlock on the back door, taking her time so the old door wouldn't squeak too loudly. She'd made sure no one was lurking around. She'd walked the block twice before entering through the courtyard. Glancing around, she didn't see any signs of life. But the sun was coming up. She could see the first pinkish-golden rays through the trees beyond the surrounding buildings.

Once she got the door open, she tiptoed inside and shut it. The lock was still broken and she couldn't padlock it from the inside, so she propped an old chair against it. She'd hear someone if they tried to come that way. Then she followed the boxes sitting in front of the mock wall and with a grunt and a shove, she moved the boxes away, then clicked on the panel.

The wall swung back to reveal a small staircase.

Esther took the stairs, then unlocked the door to the apartment. The rooms smelled musty. Dust balls danced in the early-morning sun streaming through the old linen sheers. No one had been here in days.

She'd have plenty of time to search her father's office in the back and hopefully be home before Cullen noticed she'd left.

Cullen parked Esther's car in the public parking lot near the river and made his way to Royal Street, passing a sleepy-looking Jackson Square and the looming St. Louis Cathedral. To be safe, he hurried across the square back to Decatur and went around the square then took Anna Street to double back to Royal.

So far, so good.

Looking up and down Bourbon, he slipped into the back alley of Carlisle Collectibles, then made his way to the corner of the old shed. From there, he watched the back door and saw that the padlock had been removed.

Someone was inside.

He was about to hurry to the door and go in when he spotted a figure moving behind the bougainvillea vine.

If Esther was alone in there, it wouldn't be for long.

She had some early-morning company already.

After checking the kitchen and living area and the bedroom and bath, Esther headed to the middle room that her father had turned into his private office once she moved out.

The room was dark, but she didn't dare turn on a lamp. She'd brought a tiny penlight instead. She used that to check on files and push through drawers. Working her way through years of documents that involved designer antique furniture and expensive estate jewelry, she finally let out a sigh.

Had her father left anything about the diamond here?

Then she glanced down underneath the big desk and saw what she should have remembered from her childhood. The desk had a hidden door on one side, underneath the open middle. Only Esther and her father knew about the door. Esther went down on her knees, her little light shining on a tarnished silver doorknob. She needed a key. And she guessed that key would be on the big ring she kept in her purse.

She was crossing the room when she heard a noise downstairs. Someone was at the back door.

Cullen watched as the shadowy figure jiggled the door. The man looked around, then tried again, shoving against the heavy wood. Esther must have blocked it.

Smart woman.

Cullen wasn't about to let this culprit inside, so he shadowed the corners, staying behind bushes, and made his way to the building. But before he could grab the intruder, the man managed to shove the door open enough to get inside.

Cullen watched, his heart pumping fear for Esther, while the figure disappeared into the building. Not wasting a minute, Cullen dashed toward the open door and squeezed his way past the chair that had been holding it.

Esther stayed under the desk. It was the safest place for her right now. Looking around, she tried to find some sort of weapon. But the only thing she saw was her father's old leather office chair. She could shove that toward someone and maybe knock them down.

Sweating, her spine tingling with both cold and hot shivers, she curled up underneath the big desk, her backbone pressing against the doorknob to the hidden cabinet. She didn't dare move, didn't dare inhale a breath.

What had she been thinking, coming here alone in the early morning? She'd thought she'd be safe on a Sunday morning. She should have realized she wasn't safe and she might not ever be until this was over.

Her need to outsmart Cullen and find that diamond had driven her to this. Esther closed her eyes and prayed for her life.

Cullen slipped into the hallway. Where had the intruder gone? He held a breath, then turned and saw the stairs leading to the second floor. Surely, Esther was up there. Did she know someone was about to join her? If she'd planned to meet someone here, she wouldn't have wedged that chair against the door.

Cullen heard footsteps up the stairs and started that way. He had to do something to stop this. Esther might be in serious trouble.

Esther prayed the intruder would ignore the desk drawers and go away. There didn't seem to be anything here anyway.

When she heard footsteps coming up the stairs, she knew she'd made a terrible mistake coming here alone. Then she remembered the letter opener her father kept on the desk.

Slowly, she scooted out and slid a hand up on the desk, her fingers grasping for the intricate silver-handled weapon.

She found it, her hand curling around the stiletto blade before footsteps started shuffling toward the office.

Cullen watched the man head for the open door of the apartment. Frantically searching for a weapon, he saw a fleur-de-lis bookend, one of a set, and grabbed it.

He intended to defend Esther, even though he was so furious at her right now, he could spit nails. But whoever this was seemed to know she was up there.

He'd made it inside the door when Esther came charging out from under a big desk in the corner, holding a slender silver blade in her right hand, a warrior woman scream emitting from her pretty little mouth.

The intruder threw up his hands to protect himself. "Esther!"

Cullen lifted the bookend, determined to get the man away from Esther.

Esther screamed again, this time to Cullen. "Stop. No! Cullen, don't hurt Mr. Reynolds."

FOURTEEN

"Mr. Reynolds? From next door?"

Mr. Reynolds turned, his plump hands up in the air, his bald head flushed with perspiration. "I'm so sorry. I didn't mean to scare anyone. I saw Esther and I was out back feeding the pigeons so I wanted to check on her."

"Did you think of knocking and calling out?" Cullen asked, his hand still gripping the fleur-de-lis. And he didn't remember seeing any pigeons.

"I was afraid I'd bring attention to myself if I made a racket," the frightened man said on a stutter. "I didn't want people to think she was open for business." He turned back to Esther, then flapped his arms wide. "Esther and I do this all the time, especially if we're both working early or late."

"It's true," Esther said. "We sometimes have Sunday morning breakfast together." She threw down the letter opener, then wiped her hands. "I'm sorry, Mr. Reynolds. It's been a crazy week and my nerves are shot."

"I understand, dear. Robberies leave all of us feeling defenseless. Which is one reason I wanted to check on you." He gave Cullen another appraising look. "Besides, what are you doing here?"

"He's a friend," Esther said on a rush of breath, her hand waving in dismissal.

"Really?" Mr. Reynolds didn't look convinced. "He never mentioned that to me when he bought the Remington."

"Didn't see a reason to do so," Cullen retorted.

Cullen didn't trust the plump shop owner or his beady-eyed wife. But then, he didn't really trust anyone right now.

Including Esther.

"I should go," the older man said, a sheepish expression on his puffy face. "We'll have breakfast another day."

"I'm so sorry," Esther said again. "I was going through some paperwork. I haven't had a chance to get up here this week and, well, I couldn't sleep."

Cullen saw the pleading look in her eyes. Should he believe her? She'd come here without him for a reason. He needed to hear that reason.

"Neither could I," he admitted, relief slamming against regret inside his stomach. "I was worried about you."

"I should go," Mr. Reynolds said again, backing out of the room. "I could bring coffee and beignets, help you look around."

"Why would you need to do that?" Cullen asked, still suspicious.

Esther sent him an annoyed look, then turned to Mr. Reynolds. "That's awfully nice, but—"

But the older man looked affronted. "I mean, if Esther is trying to figure out who keeps targeting her—"

"Have you seen anyone over here since yesterday?" Esther asked, her gaze slamming into Cullen's.

"No. Nothing that stands out," Mr. Reynolds replied. "I did see a couple of window shoppers around eight-thirty last night. They stood at the window looking in for a long time."

"Men?" Cullen asked.

"A man and a woman," the other man retorted. "Nice-looking young couple."

Esther let out a sigh. "We're beginning to suspect normal people."

"Normal people are criminals, too," Cullen pointed out, his gaze sliding over Mr. Reynolds.

"I guess I should let you carry on. I've had enough excitement for one morning. I'm glad you're okay, Esther. And now that I see you have a proper escort, I'll go back to my place."

"Thank you so much, Mr. Reynolds. Take care."

He brushed by Cullen with a daring look.

Cullen waited a couple of breaths, then crossed the room. "Have you lost your mind, coming here without me?"

"I don't have to check with you when I want to come to my own store," Esther replied. Then she lowered her head. "It was stupid on my part, however."

"You can't imagine." Cullen fingered his hair. "When I realized you were gone, I...I couldn't think beyond finding you." He grabbed her by the shoulders. "I feel responsible for you. Don't do that again, okay?"

"You *aren't* responsible for me." Esther gazed up at him with those vivid golden-honey eyes. "I'm not used to having someone shadow me day and night, Cullen. I deliberately came here alone to defy that notion. I didn't want you to know I'd been up here. I needed some time to absorb all of this."

Cullen had to admire that stoic confession. He almost milked it just to teach her a lesson, but the embarrassment in her pretty eyes stopped him. "Really, now? I would have never guessed that, luv." Then he dropped his hands away from her, thinking he'd like to either kiss her good and proper or shake her silly. "It's lucky for me I figured out about this place after you let something slip last night. I had to believe I'd find you here."

"And so you did. Some covert operator I am. I'm not good at covert espionage."

He almost smiled at her terminology. "Is that what you think this is?"

"Well, isn't it? Someone's out to get someone else. We're all out to get that infernal diamond." She stared down at the

desk pad. "I'm used to showing people fine china and exquisite crystal. I deal in period-piece artwork and high-back
sofas and toy soldiers, things that bring people joy. I'm not
used to being chased and stalked and shot at." She stopped,
gave him a lost look. "I'm certainly not used to you."

He grabbed her close, so glad that she hadn't been hurt
he had to take a deep breath. "Esther, you…you're a brave
woman, but these people are serious and they are dangerous.
If they'd found you here alone—"

"I know." She hugged him as if she didn't want to let go.
"I was so scared, I hid under the desk." Then she pulled back.
"I thought I could do this on my own, find something to lead
me to the diamond—"

"Before I found it," he finished. "I've corrupted you, too."

"No, you haven't," she replied, defending his honor before her own. "I…I thought I had a chance, but I need you
to help me, Cullen. We need to work together. I guess I have
to accept that."

He tugged her back. "I'd like nothing more, darlin'."

Esther nodded against his chest. "I might have found something."

"Best news I've heard all morning," Cullen said. "Show
me."

She stepped toward the desk. "I need to find my keys, but
there is a secret drawer underneath my father's old desk. I'd
forgotten."

Cullen went to look while she found the key. "Are you sure
it needs a key to open?"

She nodded, her key ring jingling. "Yes. I remember watching my father lock it up at night. I never knew what he kept
in here, but I used to hide underneath the desk and turn that
antique knob. It wouldn't open without the key." She held up
a slim, old-fashioned Victorian-style key. "And I think this
is the one."

Esther sat in the chair and watched as Cullen bent down

on his knees and forced the key into the lock. "It's a fit," he said over his shoulder. Then he turned it.

She heard a click. "It worked."

Cullen unrolled his body from under the desk. "Why don't you look?"

Esther fell down on her knees and opened the tiny door. "Papers," she said, excitement coloring her words. She grabbed at the stack and pulled some out. "Letters. Maybe your letters to him. I knew I'd find them somewhere."

Cullen sank onto the chair and pushed it away from the desk. "This is why you snuck out of the house? You wanted to find *my* letters to your father?"

"Sure," she said, digging out more papers. "I thought I might pick up more clues."

"I didn't write clues," Cullen replied, obviously uncomfortable with this new discovery. "I only discussed possibilities. Nothing in there. You'd be bored to tears."

Esther saw another sealed folder and glanced down. Her father's concise handwriting jumped out at her.

Esther—For Your Eyes Only.

She put the folder underneath some of the loose papers and cleared the little drawer, then stood up, her Cullen radar beeping a warning. "Is there something in these letters I shouldn't see?"

Cullen stood and started pacing. "No, not really. It's that... I mean, the letters I wrote back to your father are more personal in nature. I only wrote back because I found him charming and interesting. I would have much rather corresponded by email."

"Maybe you did and you're not telling me."

"We're back to that." He pointed a finger at her. "You left the house and put yourself in danger. I still can't believe—"

"I needed some downtime!" she shouted. "I needed to breathe, to think, to...find some answers."

"You can do that, but not alone." He glanced around the

apartment. "And not here. And why didn't you tell me about this place?"

She shook her head. "This was my father's home, Cullen. I have a hard time coming up here as it is, let alone bringing a stranger up here."

"I didn't think I was a stranger."

"You're not, not really. But I wanted to see if coming in here would help me remember something, anything."

"And did it?"

"I only remember how lonely he was here. How he forced me to live in the dorm at Tulane when I wanted to be here."

Cullen filled the space between them. Crushing her close, he stepped back long enough to take the papers from her and drop them on the desk. Esther went into his arms, her gaze locked on the white letter-sized envelope she'd found.

"We should go," she said, lifting her head to stare at Cullen. "I'm sorry I scared everyone."

"You don't need to figure me out. My letters to him were not that important."

"Oh, really? Well, I think I do need to figure you out. You're an interesting man, a well-educated man with good intentions that involve bad decisions. I'd like to see what makes you tick."

"You know my intentions already. Besides, finding that diamond is what makes me tick," he said, his hands dropping to his side. "Let's see what your father left in this desk, then I'll get you out of here."

Esther grabbed the letters and papers. She wondered if the man was actually saying a prayer. "I'll make some coffee."

"I'll secure the door."

He stomped out, giving her time to check the loose letters. But none of them were from Cullen. Could they be in the sealed envelope? She quickly hid the sealed envelope in her tote, then skimmed over the other papers.

But she still wondered what else Cullen might be hiding.

After placing the stack on the tiny kitchen table, she headed to the efficiency kitchen and found the coffee and an unopened box of oatmeal cookies. Breakfast, for now.

Cullen came back, then eyed the documents with a definite aversion. "Find anything interesting?"

"Relax, you're safe," Esther said. "But you can save both of us time by telling me now if there's something else I need to know."

"I don't like to talk about my personal life."

"Oh, okay. Right. You get to know everything about me, but you're not willing to open up. Typical man."

"What's that supposed to mean?"

"Men—they clam up, stay silent, never show their true feelings. My father was that way at times and so are you."

The coffee bubbled. While she brewed.

"You know this about me already?"

"I can see, Cullen. I'm not blind. The only challenge you run from is the emotional kind. You're so afraid I might actually see into your black soul, you almost bolted out of here. Am I right?"

"Maybe." He put his hands in the pockets of his jeans. "I'm not used to you, either, Esther."

His words floored her, but the dejected look on his face did her in. What did she care about his black heart? What did she care that he wouldn't stay around after he'd found what he'd come for?

"Let's focus on the diamond and the clues," she said. Then she tore into the cookies. "Want a snack?"

Cullen took two. "I'm starving."

"Help me with this and then we'll walk down to the Café du Monde and get some real coffee and some beignets."

"You told Mr. Reynolds we were going to church."

"We should," she replied. "But I'm afraid someone else might get hurt. I won't bring danger into my own church. So you can relax on that matter."

"Deal," he said, shaking her hand. "Let's see what you found underneath that desk."

Esther felt the tingling awareness of his touch all the way up her arm. And too late, she remembered this really was a very tiny apartment.

FIFTEEN

"As hideouts go, this isn't bad," Cullen said. He rather enjoyed the intimate little pied-à-terre, but his heart was still racing from discovering Esther gone. "Small and easy to exit. And the jumping-over-the-balcony thing might be fun."

Esther moved around the desk, her eyes wide, her expression unsure. "That door sticks and I don't intend to jump off the balcony. Let's see what we can find."

Cullen followed close so he could enjoy her floral scent. Now that he knew she was okay, he was filled with an odd euphoric glee. And an odd need to keep her tucked away. "We could stay hidden here indefinitely."

"Yes, that would really solve our problems." Her hands fluttered through the stack of files. She was obviously still shaken, too. "My father left some research notes at least. Let's see what they say."

He leaned close, touched a hand to her hair, his imagination thinking of nice ways to solve all of their issues. "Very cozy up here. No one to bother us. No one trying to kill us—if we rule out Mr. Reynolds, of course."

She gave him a look of disbelief. "He's harmless. We scared the poor man." Sinking down on the chair, she said, "We need to recheck the list."

Cullen sat on the desk, disappointed that she wasn't falling for his charms—and surprised that he wanted to stop and flirt a bit. They had urgent business and now all he wanted to do was dally. Delayed reaction to all this excitement. "We have all day."

Esther pushed around to stare up at him. "No, we don't, so stop distracting me. I was halfway serious about attending church, but I don't want to expose others to this threat."

That killed his mood. Defeated, but not nearly done, he stood up. "I'd never agreed to go to church with you anyway."

"Afraid the church beams might cave in?"

"I didn't say that."

"That look of utter fear on your face gave you away. Why don't you like worship, Cullen?"

"I never said I didn't like worship. I have a strong faith connection." He'd been in some of the most beautiful cathedral and churches in the world. But memories from childhood echoed all around him, shouting against all that faith. His father had been a faithful man. And a roaring drunk who beat his wife and children.

She looked worried. "Then what's wrong?"

He hit a hand on the desk, giving up on any amorous attempts to get next to her. "What's wrong? We can't stop in the middle of a diamond heist and sing hymns, Esther. It's dangerous for you, even in a church and, yes, you're wise to recognize that. I panicked when I woke up and couldn't find you. I need a minute to catch my breath."

"That's your excuse? Please! You were willing to stay here indefinitely. We don't have indefinite time. We don't have very much time at all."

"All the more reason to get on with it, then," he said, holding his hands in fists to keep from hugging her close.

"We could use some prayer, at least."

She was right, of course. He needed to focus on what needed to be done, and fast. "You pray and I'll figure out the rest."

She shook her head. "Why are you being so wishy-washy

on this? One minute, you want to slow down and the next, you're all fired up."

"Please listen to me," he said, grabbing her by the arm, hoping to make her see reason. "I'm relieved you're in one piece. But I'm ready to start acting on some of these clues. The sooner we get this solved, the safer you will be."

"And the sooner you can be gone, right?"

He stood back, shock changing to acceptance. "Well, yes. But right now I'm trying to protect you."

She stared him down, her arms crossed in protest mode. "Oh, all right. But later, Cullen, we're going to discuss your mortal fear of anything personal or spiritual. Sit down and we'll go over the clues again and see what we can add."

He let out a long sigh. Now they were getting somewhere. His mind completely clear, Cullen wanted this over so he could be on his way. He was becoming too involved and interested. He didn't do involved and interested. Unless, of course, it would produce financial reward and recognition. Those things had been important before he'd met Esther. Maybe he did need to sit down and have a long talk with the Lord.

Because even though this apartment might be cozy and private, it felt way too small for him right now.

"We need to go to the zoo," Esther said an hour later.

Cullen's shocked look was almost comical. "Excuse me?"

"Think about it," she said, tapping her pen on her notes. "All this talk about birds and snakes in the valley. And he did mention the white tigers. The Audubon Zoo is a good place to start."

He gave her a twisted frown. "Based on what you just said?"

"Based on how my father used to take me there and based on how he mentions that in the letters. Of course, it's changed a lot. Everything's been updated and improved. There is a fabulous bird aviary there now. Not to mention the reptile exhibit. There's even a swamp area. If we don't find anything, at least we'll be inspired."

"The zoo? You want to go to the zoo?"

Esther couldn't explain it, but she had feeling. "My father rarely left New Orleans. He couldn't have survived a day in a muggy, bug-infested swamp, digging for diamonds. That makes me believe he thought the diamond wasn't out in the wilds of Louisiana, but maybe right here in the city somewhere."

Cullen shook his head. "Lafitte supposedly had the foresight to bury the diamond in the Atchafalaya Basin or somewhere near the bay. I don't see what that has to do with the zoo."

"Yes, and you think my father found it. Maybe he hid it again. There might be something in the zoo he wanted us to see, something in one of the displays that could trigger the location. Most of the marshlands and swamps have disappeared or changed completely, not to mention all the construction from oil rigs and pipelines. For all we know, someone found the diamond or it's lost forever. We'd need a local guide to navigate us through the marshlands and barrier islands."

"You do have a point. The Hope Diamond was lost and found over several hundred years."

"Exactly. And that might be why Father mentioned that particular diamond, too."

"Your mind amazes me," he said, grabbing another cookie. "The zoo? Seriously?" He shrugged. "But you might be on to something since you remember going there as a child. He'd figure you'd have fond memories of those times. If he made a point to mention the zoo, then you might remember something that I would have completely skimmed over."

"I've thought about it," Esther replied. "One thing I do know is how my father's analytical mind worked. He put these things in the letters for a reason. The underlining and the exclamations—that's how he always remembered things. He left notes all over the shop with the same type of highlights. He'd underline something twice if it was really important."

"I get that, but what does that have to do with the zoo?"

"I can't explain exactly, except that when I put several things together with his mention of the white tigers, some of the clues stood out enough to make me think of the zoo."

"Monkeys? Giraffes? Lions?"

"No. Hear me out. He mentions falcons, blue herons, snakes and the Orange River in Africa. He compares the Orange to the Mississippi, then goes on to mention Alexander Bay near the sea where the Orange empties, and then he describes Barataria Bay and how it's caught between the Mississippi and all the bayous. Why would he do that?"

Cullen shrugged. "I have no idea, except that both the Orange and the Mississippi are the longest rivers on their respective continents, I believe. And the Orange is known for its diamond regions. But the Mississippi?"

"Might also have one rather large diamond somewhere near it." She bobbed her head. "He mentions India as the source of great diamonds, which is pretty common knowledge. Then he says something in one of the letters about the Mayan Ruins and jaguars in the jungle and how he's enjoyed the new exhibits at the zoo. The zoo has a Mayan Ruins exhibit and the Jaguar Jungle."

She dropped her notes, then gazed around the apartment. "His ramblings sometimes make no sense and my father always made sense. His tone changes from the first letters to the last few letters, almost as he's become confused. Couple all of these odd mentions with the birds he keeps referring to, and, well, we can either explore millions of miles of swamp or we can check the zoo first. So do you have any better ideas?"

"No, I don't. It's a stretch, but it beats sitting around on me bum, I guess." He grabbed her hand. "I've always wanted to see the New Orleans zoo. Let's go."

* * *

They had a while before the zoo opened so they walked to the Café du Monde. Careful to check for anybody who might be watching, Cullen tried to relax and enjoy the sweet taste of beignets and powdered sugar. And being with Esther. Thankful that she hadn't forced him to head to the St. Louis Cathedral or some quaint chapel, Cullen was happy to have a few minutes to scan the crowds.

But he didn't like being so exposed and he didn't like where this new idea was going. Esther had picked up on how her father had changed from the beginning letters to the last few letters. When Cullen had first noticed that shift, he'd chalked it up to early dementia. Should he tell her his other theory on that?

Not yet. Right now, he listened to her thoughts on the zoo connection and began to think she might be right.

"Your father used to send you on scavenger hunts around the city, right?"

"Yes. And that's what this feels like. He's pointing me to the zoo for a reason."

"But what then? Would he leave an obvious clue or would he expect you to keep searching?"

"I don't know. I don't know why he felt he had to write you instead of telling me these things."

Cullen understood this part of the puzzle, at least. "He was trying to protect you. I was his insurance policy. He knew I had experience and that I was qualified, and that I wouldn't be able to resist coming here, whether he was alive or not. And I believe he somehow stumbled on my connection with Hogan." He didn't add that he'd wanted to meet the woman Jefferson Carlisle had described in such glowing terms, either. He'd never considered that he'd begin to have feelings for her.

They finished their meal and started toward the street-car stop. Esther touched a hand to Cullen's arm. "But did he sense he was dying? Is that why he wanted you to come to New Orleans?"

Hurrying to follow her to the St. Charles Avenue streetcar, Cullen wondered if he should comment on that. Would she believe him if he told her his suspicions? And how could he prove that he was pretty sure someone had done something to cause her father's heart attack? Had it been poison, maybe?

"Esther, refresh my memory on some of your father's comments," he said, holding her elbow and cutting his gaze left and right to make sure they weren't being followed. So far, everyone looked disinterested. But that could be a ploy.

Esther kept watching, too. "What would you like to know?"

"How many times does he mention poison in the letters?"

She stopped when they reached the streetcar pickup past the corner of Royal and Canal. "Why do you ask that?"

"I'm trying to put things together, same as you."

After they were settled into their seat, she turned to him. "As far as I can remember, only a couple. He talked about workers being warned not to swallow the diamonds because they were poisonous. But a lot of people centuries ago thought diamonds were actually good for medicinal reasons, too. Holding one in the hand, for example, might ward off evil or an illness. Or in the case of the Blue Hope Diamond, bring nothing but a curse. Silly, right?"

"Hmm. Diamonds can make honorable men lose all honor." Cullen thought about the possibility of poison. "Didn't he use the word *ingested* a few times?"

"Yes, yes, he did. What are you getting at?"

Cullen watched as the streetcar whirled by the stately homes lining St. Charles. "I can't be sure. But I'm concerned about the tone you picked up on in your father's final letters. Did they seem a bit desperate?"

Shock colored her eyes. "Did you think that?"

"I didn't put it together until you figured out he might be

trying to send us a message. He underlined *ingested* and *poison* in some of the letters."

"Cullen, you're scaring me."

"Was there an autopsy?"

"Yes. I called 911 and they tried to revive him at the scene. But it was too late. I told them he had heart trouble. And that's what was determined, a heart attack."

Cullen leaned in so only she would hear. "There are some poisons that can't be detected until it's too late."

"Why didn't you tell me this before?"

"You thought he'd died of natural causes so I didn't want to press the issue. But now that you've noticed the difference in the letters, I'm beginning to think I might be right."

Esther stared ahead, watching as the streetcar bounced along, the wind from the open windows lifting her hair away from her face. "That would mean someone who knew us is involved in this."

"Yes, or someone who pretended to be a friend managed to poison your father. After we check out the zoo, we need to do some research on that possibility, too."

They exited the streetcar at the Audubon Park stop. Cullen glanced back, watching the other passengers. Mostly families out for a day at the zoo. Some elderly people. Young couples.

"I think we're safe so far."

But Esther wasn't listening. "Why didn't he tell me he was so sick?"

"Did you notice anything odd during his last months?"

"He was tired more. He went to the doctor for regular check-ups. But maybe he didn't suspect anything out of the ordinary." She glanced around at the stately oak trees lining the park entrance. "Or maybe it only took one dose. If this is true, then I'm a part of this. I should have noticed, should have helped him."

Cullen pulled her to the side. "Esther, don't think that way. I only told you so we could find a way to prove it and also find out who's behind this. It might not be Charles Hogan. It could be someone close to you and your father instead."

She looked up at him, her eyes misty and wide. "Or it could be someone who's connected to both."

SIXTEEN

The Audubon Zoo was crowded with tourists on a nice day like today. But Cullen couldn't relax. He kept looking over his shoulder.

Esther seemed to feel his tension. She cut her gaze left and right and held tightly to her tote bag. "We've got nothing. No clues, no hints, nothing. Maybe I was wrong."

Cullen tugged her underneath the shade of an ancient live oak covered with Spanish moss. "At least we're together. I think I'll always have fond memories of the orangutans and spider monkeys."

"Funny." Esther smiled up at him, her blush shining brightly against her creamy skin. "They were cute, weren't they?"

"There's that smile," he said, his heart warming with something that shined like a bright jewel. "Yes, but that orangutan took an immediate liking to you and I'm so jealous. I'll fight him for you." He touched a hand to her hair. "So this wasn't an entire waste. I have you close and you're safe."

Esther leaned into his embrace, the gentle flush continuing down her skin. "This is crazy. Instead of enjoying this beautiful day, we're on pins and needles and searching for the proverbial diamond in a haystack." She sighed, a look of longing in her eyes. "Why couldn't we have met under normal circumstances, Cullen?"

"Would you have given me the time of day?"

She looked startled. "I don't know. You're not my type. I don't actually have a type. I kind of gave up on having a relationship." She shrugged. "My dad was a loner, a complex man who lost the love of his life. That terrifies me to the point I'm afraid to seek out any type of intimacy."

"Do I scare you?" he asked, determined to show her his kind of intimacy. Cullen could see the terror in her eyes, but he wanted to wipe it away, to calm all her fears.

But then, he *was* the kind of man her father had probably warned Esther about. Which didn't make a bit of sense. Her father had practically handpicked Cullen to find—or rather, rediscover—that diamond and to protect his daughter, too.

What did you see in me, Mr. Carlisle, that made you write all those letters? Letters that had caused Cullen to care, to dream, to hope. And it wasn't about the diamond anymore.

Esther gave him a look that told him of her fear, a look that brought him out of his musings. "Yes, you scare me, but I scare myself even more when I'm around you. You make me reckless and daring, and I'm not those things."

He took her hand, squeezed it. "You are those things. You don't know that yet."

She smiled, a soft bittersweet smile that tore at his guarded heart. "I'm caught up in this diamond tale. I don't want it to control me. And I'm not so sure I want you to do that, either."

Cullen tugged her along the path. "Ah, there's your real fear, then. Let's change the subject. What did we accomplish, coming here?"

"I'm not sure," she admitted. "I have all these thoughts in my head as if the answer is right here and I can't grasp it. I've read so many letters I can remember each tiny detail, but I'm sure something else is there, glaring at me."

"The elephant exhibit was enlightening," he replied, hoping to trigger some memories. "And how about those white tigers and white alligators. You were so keen on the tigers.

Can't say I've seen such animals before. So rare, and so beautiful."

"White," she said, mumbling against his neck, her warm breath tickling him. "I thought the tigers would remind me. White animals. We also saw white owls and a white falcon, remember?"

"Yes, that's the color," Cullen replied, happy to have her lips so close to his skin. Her pretty, pouting, kissable lips.

She pulled away, her eyes doing that golden-lioness thing. "White, Cullen."

Here we go again, Cullen thought. Well, he had come here for her help. But he was seriously beginning to doubt her sanity. And his. In spite of that, he loved how her mind worked. The woman wouldn't stop till she had this thing figured out. All the more reason for him to stick close. Would he hurt her, or would he wind up being the one who ran away in terror?

"What are you thinking, luv?"

"A white rock." She found a bench and sank down, then started pulling letters out. "The white rock," she repeated. "Of course!"

Cullen plopped down beside her. "I don't recall seeing a white rock in the zoo."

She gave him a covert glance. "I didn't pick up on it before. My father used to mention a large white rock to me. He would make up these elaborate stories and they'd usually end with the princess in a white dress finding the white rock in the middle of the swamp. And…in the story, he talked about the white alligators and the white tigers with the *chocolate* stripes."

She had Cullen's attention now. "Go on."

"We checked every exhibit here, even the albino alligators and the white tigers. I was so engrossed in watching the tigers, I didn't think about the meaning. And I've always loved Rex and Zulu, so it makes perfect sense."

Cullen frowned. "Excuse me?"

"The white tigers, remember. They're brothers and those are their names—they were named after Mardi Gras krewes."

"I remember him talking about the stories he used to tell you, but I thought that was the ramblings of a doting father. I suppose it could be related."

"No, he didn't mention the tigers by name, but he did mention them in one letter. A more recent letter. That's odd. But then, this whole thing is odd."

She shook her head, then glanced down at the letters and the notes she'd taken as they toured the exhibits. "He mentioned so many things about the zoo, and I didn't even connect on the zoo and the animals with the white rock."

She tore through the pages written by her father. "I'd have to find the letter, but he wrote something about 'the story I used to tell my daughter—the white tale' when he talked about the white falcon and the tigers."

She read through a couple of sheets. While she did Cullen kept watch, praying no one was lurking about or following their every move. If she was really on to something, someone could easily snatch her right from under his eyes.

"I found it," Esther said on a loud whisper. "Listen."

She read, "'When Esther was in grammar school, I used to tell her a made-up story about the *White Swamp* and the *White Rock*. She was the princess in my stories—in her white dress, her bright hair long and flowing. A beautiful child who walked through the swamp with a *white falcon* on her arm and two *white tigers* that protected her.'"

Esther stopped, tears in her eyes. "He must have thought I'd come here and…see the white tigers and remember. I was fascinated by them when they first came to the zoo. I was younger then, of course, but still…why didn't I remember right away?"

Cullen's heart ached for the lost little girl. "Esther, your father sure was counting on you for a lot. And me, too, I think. I still don't know why he decided to tell me these elaborate tales, but it did bring me to you. I don't want you to be disappointed, though. Are you sure you're not putting things together to make this work?"

She dashed at tears. "What if that's what he wanted? He taught me to think—to arrange things together that didn't seem to match. To look beyond the obvious clues and see what was right there in front of my eyes. And Rex and Zulu were right there."

Cullen wanted to understand the dynamics between Esther and her father. He'd never had that kind of relationship with his dad. And he'd often wished for it when he read over her father's strange, rambling letters. "I thought you two never talked that much."

"We didn't. Not about the one emotional issue that held us apart—my mother's death when I was born." She shrugged, pushed at loose strands of hair, her eyes going dark. "But he always read me these crazy, adventurous stories, and some nights he'd sit there and tell me these made-up stories. I lived for those nights because it was the only time he came alive. I think it was his way of avoiding the story I wanted to hear—the one about my mother and their life together. Was he preparing me even then?"

"That's a large assumption," Cullen replied, seeing her pain. "But at this point, I can go with anything. The man started a long correspondence with me after…" Cullen wanted to tell her more, but held back. Not yet. Not now.

She bobbed her head. "And it's all falling into place. He studied Lafitte's history and told me stories about the pirate. But as I got older, he began to focus more on the chocolate diamond." She grabbed Cullen by the lapels, her golden-brown eyes sparkling with hope. "I tuned him out, Cullen. I stopped listening because I thought it was a wild-goose chase. How could I do that to my father? How?"

Cullen clutched her hands. "You had no idea I'd come here, Esther, or that the diamond might actually be real. Your father told you fairy tales to hide the reality of things. How can we know you're on the right path even now?"

"Because, even though I tried so hard to distance myself from what I thought was a fantastical dream, somehow in my subconscious, I registered a lot of this information."

"And now because of these letters, it's all coming back?"

"Yes, even with the clues he so haphazardly left in his letters. I remember him talking about the Orange River and the Mississippi River. And about the swamps and the barrier islands. And the birds—he loved Louisiana birds almost as much as John James Audubon did. The herons, the egrets, the ospreys and white falcons, the white owl. I have to go back and look over that bird book from my childhood. I must have missed something."

"It's too dangerous."

"It's still my home. And I need that book."

Cullen wanted to get excited but, honestly, this was like spinning in circles. Esther was becoming as obsessed with this as the rest of them. "But I thought the clues were here in the zoo?"

"No," she said, taking him by the hand to hurry to the nearest exit. "Coming to the zoo was a way for me to remember. He knew how much I loved this place as a child. He taught me to look for all the clues, to never give up. And I believe one of the clues is in that childhood book." She turned toward him as they approached the park. "Rex and Zulu are a big clue—white tigers with chocolate stripes." Then she grinned and grabbed Cullen's hand. "I think I know where the white rock might be, Cullen."

Cullen's heart thumped like a drum against his rib cage. He glanced back, then took her arm. And that's when he saw the man watching them.

"Esther, I think we've been discovered. Remember the big goon with the large nose—he pressed it against the glass of the old shed behind the shop?"

"Yes." She didn't turn to look, but Cullen saw the anger and fear in her eyes.

"He's behind us and he seems to be leaving the zoo."

Esther's phone rang as they hurried through Audubon Park. The wind was whipping around them. The massive live oaks swayed, the gray-white Spanish moss covering them like a veil suddenly becoming sinister and mysterious. Cullen heard thunder off in the distance.

"It's Ted," she said before answering the call. "He might have some information."

"Now?" Cullen asked, dragging her along. "You know we're being followed, right?"

"Yes, but I need to take the call. He'll keep calling."

Cullen believed that. "Walk and talk. Maybe our friend will think you're calling the police."

"Hello?" She put it on speaker, so Cullen could hear but held it close.

Cullen dragged her through the great oaks near the pond where several white swans moved in elegant symmetry across the dark water. The skies turned dark and ominous.

"You wanted me to dig around, remember?" Ted said.

"Yes. What did you find?"

Esther held up a hand for Cullen to stop. He motioned to an outcropping of banana fronds near a fountain and they headed that way. They'd be partially hidden and he could check out the park in all directions.

"Hurry." Cullen shoved her back into the big green leaves while he kept an eye on the surrounding grounds. "We've lost him for now."

"Esther, what's going on? Where are you?"

"Uh, outside. Reception's bad."

After Cullen gave her the go-ahead she went back to the call. "Ted? Did you find anything?"

"Not much," Ted replied. "I don't get how all these underlined words can mean anything. You know how eccentric Mr. Jefferson was. I think he got off on tangents in his writings, same as when he'd get all excited talking to a customer. Remember how he'd wander from one subject to the next?"

"Yes, I understand," she said, her eyes ever watchful, disappointment echoing through her response. "So you can't see a pattern between any of those things?"

Apparently, she'd enlisted her trusty sidekick to help and Ted had come up empty. Somehow, that bothered Cullen on so many levels. He didn't trust Ted and he didn't trust portly Mr. Reynolds or the local police. He was beginning not even to trust himself. Especially since he was so close to abandoning the infernal diamond so he could sweep Esther up in his arms and claim her in the same way he imagined Lafitte claiming a prize.

Was Esther the real prize here? Was that the biggest clue her father had left? Cullen pushed that out of his mind so he could listen to the conversation with one ear and watch the street with both eyes.

"I mean, if these are supposed to be clues, they are very random," Ted said. "The Blue Hope was bigger than the Levi-Lafitte chocolate, but that could be considered a comparison, I guess. Something to think about—the Hope Diamond changed hands a lot. And all this about birds—what does that have to do with finding the chocolate diamond? If a bird tried to swallow that thing, he'd choke to death. Maybe a porcelain or clay bird?"

Esther's eyes widened. "That's a thought. I guess I'm grasping at things to find a connection. But today—"

Cullen shook his head and held a finger to his lips.

Esther looked surprised, then nodded. "Today, I went to the shop apartment and found some more papers and files. I haven't had a chance to look through them yet, but maybe something will turn up."

"Where were they?" Ted asked, his tone more intent now.

"In the desk." She glanced at Cullen and shrugged, but thankfully, she didn't go into detail.

"Okay. Maybe you'll find something else. Let me know if I can help with anything," Ted replied. "My ankle's better so I should be back in New Orleans sometime next week."

Esther hung up and looked at Cullen. "Ted thinks I'm imagining things and maybe he's right. He doesn't see a correlation between the list I've made and any clues to finding the diamond."

"Of course he doesn't," Cullen mumbled, grumpy from too many cookies and beignets and not enough sleep or trust—and the fact that she'd turned to Ted without consulting Cullen. Not to mention, someone had probably been following them all day.

"Let's take a different route, in case Bozo picks up our trail again."

She glanced behind them. "I don't see anyone."

"I don't either, but that little chat with Ted might have cost us valuable time."

Her brows furrowed together. "You don't care for Ted, do you? You didn't want me to tell him about the white rock?"

How to answer that? Cullen tugged her between bushes and around trees with six feet wide trunks, walking backward so he could watch. "I don't know the man. He seems to worry over a lot of things I'd not worry about, but he doesn't get all worked up about finding the diamond. He dismissed your findings too quickly, if you ask me."

Esther kept walking. "No, he doesn't care about all that. Ted's an introvert. He loves his work at the shop and…" She stopped, shrugged. "And I guess he reads a lot and walks around the Quarter when he's not working."

"You mean you don't know what he does with his life?"

"It's not my business. We're like sister and brother, but I don't question him on what he does after hours."

"Do you trust him?"

"Of course, or I wouldn't have asked for his help."

"Right."

"You can't seriously think Ted's involved? He'd run at the first sign of trouble. That's why I sent him to Baton Rouge."

"Exactly. He's safe and you're here in the thick of it."

"Stop it," Esther said. "Ted is not like that. He's not a troublemaker and he doesn't care for fame or fortune."

Cullen stopped her when they reached the bird rookery. Several snowy white egrets lifted out of one of the old oaks and took flight. "Remember what I said about that diamond, Esther. It can change any man."

"That's obvious," she said, her frown indicating it had changed him. She turned and started toward the park entrance, then tossed him a glance over her shoulder.

And stopped just past the columned entrance.

"Cullen, that man is still following us."

SEVENTEEN

Cullen pushed her against the column. "We need to go back into the park."

Esther shook her head, her pulse hammering against her temple. "He's in *there*."

"But he won't do anything if we're in a crowd."

"You hope not."

"Look, he's probably been tailing us all day and he hasn't made a move yet. He's waiting until he can get us alone. We'll veer off to the right and find another way out." He glanced around the square column, then turned back to Esther, his touch protective and full of steel. "I don't see him right now, but that doesn't mean much."

"He's in there waiting, the big coward."

Cullen leaned against the stone and held her close. "For now, luv, let's pretend we're two people enjoying the beautiful day."

Esther gave him a tired frown. "Did you notice the sky?"

An angry rumble of thunder echoed as if to remind him.

"Yes. That could be to our advantage. Some people don't like getting wet." He leaned in to graze her cheek with a whisper of a kiss, then said, "On three, we take off through the park and try to get back to your apartment."

"What about the shop?"

"Not safe."

Esther waited, wishing those three-second counts with his lips against her ear could turn into a lifetime. The weather was taking a nasty turn right along with her life.

"Now," Cullen said, tugging her around.

They pivoted together and saw Bozo hurrying up the alley of old live oaks. He spotted them, then started stomping toward them, his gun down by his side.

Fat, cold raindrops hit at them. "Cullen?"

"We can make a run out of the park, or we can trick him and make him think we've gone back toward the zoo."

"But he has a gun."

"Then we'd better run fast."

Cullen pushed her into the trees, hurrying around a big fountain. A bullet pinged nearby, but a clap of thunder covered the sound of the shot.

When a shot whizzed by and hit the path, Cullen pushed her ahead of him. "Go!"

The wind picked up, scattering pine straw and flower blossoms all around them. He urged Esther off the paved pathway and shouted, "Let's head toward the golf course. Maybe I can find a golf club and stop that thug in his size-thirteen tracks."

Esther didn't look back. "Okay."

She took his hand and they ran through the rain and wind, pivoting around the trees and through the footpaths, ducking under shrubbery and hiding behind towering oaks. Cullen pulled her into a cluster of azaleas, their cotton-candy-pink blooms providing a stunning shelter. Underneath the oaks, they were somewhat protected from the weather.

"Let's see what happens next," Cullen said, holding Esther behind him near a massive trunk. "Maybe we can work our way to the golf course from here."

"Or out onto the street," Esther said. She didn't want an innocent person to get caught in the line of fire.

The big man ignored the coming storm and followed the paved path, a cell phone in one hand and his gun in the other.

He glanced around, a scowl darkening his face, then tapped a chunky finger against the phone.

"Maybe he's ordering a pizza," Cullen quipped, his hand holding Esther's.

"We should have been more careful."

"I was careful. I didn't see him at all until we started out of the zoo."

"He must have spotted us and waited."

Someone came around the corner toward the gunman. "Look," Esther gasped. "His friend looks familiar."

Cullen held her tight. "Yes, and now there are two."

"We should call the police."

Cullen thought about that. "You *are* being stalked and you've had invasions in both your workplace and your home. Maybe the authorities do need to hear everything."

"Finally, you're listening to reason," Esther said, her phone out. She covered it from the rain with her hand.

"Wait." Cullen watched the gunman and his friend. The two men were discussing something in angry voices while the wind and rain raged all around them. He couldn't make out what, but he figured it had to do with Esther and him. And that diamond. The gunman apparently wanted to continue on the path, but the other man held him back. Trouble amongst thieves?

"Cullen?" Esther nudged him. "I need to call 911."

He could be reasonable, but he wasn't stupid. "Let's go to the police station instead."

Esther frowned again. "Why?"

Cullen pointed to Tiny Tim and Big Foot. "So we can lure them out of this park and away from children." Or possibly get them alone and question them. It was a risk but better than bringing in the authorities and causing mass chaos.

Esther glanced at the men then at her phone. "I suppose that would be better than having a shoot-out here."

"Yes, luv, especially since we don't have anything to shoot back with."

They both turned back to the two men huddled together near the big fountain. And watched as the smaller one dragged Big Foot away. In the other direction.

"A change of plans."

When they heard sirens, Esther nodded her head. "Once again, someone else beat me to the punch." She sighed. "Can we go now?"

Cullen did one more thorough search of the grounds. "Yes, but you're not going back to the carriage house. Too dangerous."

"I need to find that children's book."

"I'll get you the book, don't worry."

She stared at him, shock registering on her face. "Not without me. I won't let you get shot before we find that diamond."

"And after?"

Her expression said it all. "You're on your own there."

He searched her face. "You're serious?"

"I have to talk to the police, Cullen. I've had enough of sneaking around and watching my back."

That didn't exactly answer the question, but Cullen had a gut feeling she'd protect that diamond over him any day. She was that stoic, that full of integrity.

While he was a shallow man falling fast for an amazing woman. In the middle of a diamond heist gone very wrong.

"I don't mind you filing a report, but I'm not going to let you stay in the Garden District apartment or the one over the shop until we know who's behind this."

"Well, then I guess I'm out on the street."

They heard the sirens whining to a halt.

"The cavalry has arrived," Cullen said. "Let's see if our visitors even notice."

They stayed in the shelter of the great oak, watching as

Big Foot and Tiny Tim picked up the pace and raced toward the nearest tree, both with guns drawn.

"I'm pretty sure that's the same two men who came into the shop," Esther said. "Are they working for that Hogan man?"

"Could be," Cullen said. "He has a lot of people under his thumb."

"But it could also be someone who knew my father."

"Yes. I wish I could say for sure Charles Hogan sent these men." They heard rushed footsteps. Cullen held a hand to his lips. Two uniformed officers hurried by.

"Let's go," Esther replied. "You can explain how we're supposed to get that book out of my apartment."

Cullen nodded, then said, "I have a better idea. Let's see who the police talk to."

"What makes you say that?"

They kept to the trees as they walked. When Cullen saw her shivering, he tugged Esther into the crook of his arm. "Someone is always a step ahead of us. Or behind us. In your shop. At the carriage house. Maybe even in the upstairs apartment. What if that person is the real culprit?"

"You mean, the someone who might have known my father?"

"Yes." They reached the fountain again. "Let's casually walk around and see what we see."

Esther took his hand. "It's raining."

Cullen held her close. "I won't let you melt."

"There they go!" Esther pointed as the two men ran from tree to tree, inching toward the open gate.

Cullen tugged her back off the path.

Then they heard someone calling halt. "The police," Esther said on a hiss of relief. "They ran right toward them."

But before she and Cullen could move, gunfire sounded. Big Foot was shooting at the police. The officers returned fire.

And the big man went down, his weapon flying out of his hand as he crashed to the earth.

The other man kept running and ducking behind the same bushes Cullen and Esther had used as cover.

"Stop!" the officers shouted.

Esther gave Cullen a frightened look. "One down and one to go. We need to do something."

"What do you suggest?" Cullen asked, the sound of gunfire making him think they'd do best to stay hidden.

Esther glanced around. "Tree limb."

"Trees?" Cullen watched as she grabbed a broken oak limb covered with wet, withered leaves. "Are you suggesting we use that to rustle up the bad guys?"

"We can chase him and hit him over his head."

She was already out onto the path. Amazed, Cullen hurried after her, rain pelting him with every soggy step.

"Do you want to get caught in the cross fire?" Then Cullen pointed. "There's an officer with him, Esther."

She looked disappointed but held to the limb. Cullen forced the limb out of her hands and hurried toward where Big Foot lay groaning. The officer had his phone to his ear, probably calling the paramedics.

"He doesn't look like he's trying to escape."

Esther made a dainty grunt. "I'd still like to hit him over the head with that limb."

Not wanting to argue, Cullen held her back as they approached the scene.

"Hey," the man said on a moan, "let me up."

The officer shook his head. "Sir, you've been injured. You need to be seen by a doctor."

"No doctor."

The officer pushed him back down. "You withdrew a weapon and fired shots in a public park. Injured or not, you're going to jail for discharging a weapon against a police officer."

"And for trying to shoot us," Esther said, rain running in rivulets down her face.

The officer put away his phone. "You two know this guy?"

Esther nodded. "I think he broke into my antiques shop two days ago."

The big thug looked terrified. "I don't know what you're talking about, lady."

The officer stood. "Want to explain, ma'am?"

Cullen leaned over the man. "Tell us who sent you."

The cop tapped Cullen on his wet shirt. "That's my job."

The man lay back down. He was soaked through and blood seeped out of his wounded shoulder. "I'm not talking," he said on a ragged breath.

"You folks need to go stand over there," the officer said. "My partner will take your statement."

Cullen and Esther both looked up to see a uniformed officer standing near a snack cart. But Cullen couldn't help noticing the portly man who hurried away from the scene. He was underneath an umbrella and facing away from them, but Cullen recognized him immediately.

Cullen pulled her back off the path, then shoved her behind a statue. "Esther, take a look at the man past the officer."

Esther pushed at her wet hair and stared through the gray rain. "What?" She let out a breath, then hissed, "That's Mr. Reynolds. What's he doing in the park?"

"I don't know," Cullen said. "But we're not sticking around to find out."

"But we have to give our statement," Esther replied. "We can ask him if he saw anything."

"Not here and not now."

Cullen dragged her back through the trees until they made it to the park entrance. Then he hailed a cab and got Esther away before anyone noticed.

Two hours later, Esther stood staring out the window of a French Quarter hotel, a suite complete with a sitting room with a sofa bed for Cullen and a private bed and bath for her.

He was her self-assigned bodyguard. But then, he hadn't actually left her side since this whole thing had started a few days ago.

"I want to go home," she said, whirling around from the partial view of Jackson Square. Cullen had booked the room from the taxi, then shuffled her in, ordered food and clothing and paid the bellhop a nice tip for those items as well as his discretion.

Amazing how the man had eyeballed her size and told the bellhop to bring up a nice outfit from the gift shop. Of course, Esther had yet to put on her new duds. She was wrapped in a fluffy bathrobe over her wet clothes.

Cullen was enjoying the late lunch. "Come and eat, Esther. This steak is superb. And the jambalaya looks great."

"I can't eat, Cullen. We didn't get a chance to question that thug."

"We don't need to question him," Cullen said. He got up to come and stand with her. "The police have him now. But I'm thinking he won't talk. Especially if he is one of Hogan's henchmen."

Esther shivered at that thought. "If they kill me, they'll be able to search both my home and my shop at will."

"Yes, but today they were probably hoping to kill *me* so they could take you alive."

That made her shiver even more. "I want this over with."

He turned her from the window, his hand on her chin. "You are exhausted. Come and have some tea at least. I ordered hot tea especially for you."

Esther followed him, too tired to fight. She sat down and sipped the tea. "This is good."

"Have some bread and butter. It's fresh."

She took a slice of the crusty French bread, slapped some creamy butter on it and bit into it. "Not bad."

"That's more like it," Cullen said.

"What if the police find out these men are looking for a

certain piece of jewelry worth millions of dollars and that I might have it?"

"These men won't tell the police anything."

She sipped her tea, then stared down at her plate. "I'm glad the police caught at least one of them."

Cullen nodded. "They can delve into the background of those two goons and hopefully find out things we can't."

She chewed at her bread and took another sip of tea. "Yes. But we still need to go to the police and see if we can find out who sent them. And I need to get that children's book from the carriage-house apartment."

Cullen cut into his steak and took a big bite. Then he leaned across the little bistro table. "And...you still haven't told me about the white rock. You said you think you know where it might be."

She wiped crumbs from her mouth and saw Cullen's gaze following her actions. Suddenly the fancy room became warm, too warm. "Yes, I think I might have that figured out at least."

He put down his fork, his eyes still on her face. "Tell me, then."

Trying to focus, Esther swallowed. "It's a place. Out from the city."

"In the swamp?"

"Near a swamp. I have these vague memories of going there once or twice. I have to put what we've learned into some sort of order."

"Why don't you try telling it in a story form, the way your father used to do?"

She glanced over at him, smiled. "That's a good idea. Maybe that's what he expected me to do." Then she shrugged. "I wish I could understand why he couldn't trust me."

Cullen got up and came around the table. Taking one of her hands in his, he leaned down. "You were in college during the years we wrote back and forth. Maybe this gave him something to ease his loneliness."

"He shut me out, Cullen."

"No, he let you go. I'm sure he wanted to hover and protect you, since you were his only child and his princess. But he did the best thing he knew to do—he pushed you out of the nest."

"But I wound up right back in that nest. It doesn't make sense."

"What did you dream about doing after college?"

She stared up at him, her heart warming to the genuine curiosity and concern in his eyes. "I wanted to be an artist, to create beautiful things. I moved into the townhouse, worked at the shop when I was needed. I'd planned to travel and maybe find work in a gallery or museum. Anything to do with art and books and culture. But my father seemed so lonely, I couldn't bring myself to leave New Orleans. Besides, I had friends here and my church, and I love this city."

"You stayed near the person you loved the most in the world."

"Yes."

He touched a hand to her hair, his smile warm and sure. "I think your father wanted you to enjoy your college years. He loved you, Esther. You have to see it in his letters."

"Remind me again—how did you find him?" she asked, still mystified about the odd friendship. Still wondering about Cullen's missing letters to her father.

"I first researched him and asked some questions, then he responded in kind. He saw my areas of expertise so he kept up the correspondence. I assumed he'd heard about me through one of his historical-society friends. I did a symposium on Native American mound builders in the swamps here and that's what he initially wrote about in his first couple of letters. Based on that, he agreed to discuss things with me."

"Did you mention the diamond to anyone during that time?"

"No, no, I didn't. But, Esther, your father was more than willing to discuss the diamond with me. He was excited about the prospect of discovering it."

She nudged her chin up. "Did you find that odd?"

"No. I'm used to answering questions regarding all kinds of digs—some rumored to be in certain places and some a figment of someone's imagination. And I had questions of my own. I had to find out what your father knew. And remarkably, he knew a lot."

She leaned against him, exhaustion pulling at her. "Maybe this is a little bit of both—rumors and imagination."

Cullen kissed the top of her head. "I think you need to rest a bit. When you wake up, we'll talk more."

"Okay," she said. "Thank you for the clothes."

"You're welcome. In the meantime, maybe I'll go back over the letters myself and see if I've missed anything."

"Okay."

She gathered the bag the bellhop had brought up and headed for the bathroom inside her room. Then she turned at the door. "Cullen?"

He whirled back around from the sitting room. "Yes?"

"Thank you."

"For what, luv?"

"For being there for my father. I know that sounds cliché, but he didn't have very many close friends. He must have trusted you to make you his confidant."

Cullen lowered his head but kept his eyes on her. "We had a nice relationship, yes."

He stood there staring at her and Esther felt her pulse picking up, felt the awareness flowing over her and around her. But she couldn't let go of the notion that he wasn't being completely honest with her.

"I'd better, uh, get cleaned up."

"Yes." He hesitated as if he wanted to say more.

But instead, he stalked across the doorway and grabbed

her into his arms and kissed her, his actions as solid and sure as the look of longing in his blue-gray eyes.

"What was that for?" Esther asked when he stepped back with a ragged breath.

"Good measure," he said. Then he backed into his room and shut the door between them.

EIGHTEEN

Cullen knocked on Esther's door, worried that she wasn't up yet. Even more worried that she'd left again. He'd heard her moving around during the night, but now the room was so quiet. Maybe she had been thinking the same thing he kept thinking—about kisses and dreams and longing.

He'd never stayed awake thinking of such things before.

But Esther brought out all of his protective instincts and made him wish for long nights by a fire and long walks in a misty rain back in Ireland. He wanted to take her home with him and show her his world, let her create her interesting art with him watching from a distance.

He wanted Esther—always.

And that kiss last night had sealed his fate forever.

But did she feel the same?

And how would she feel once this was over? Once she discovered the truth?

Cullen knocked again. "Esther?"

"Yes.

He opened the door a notch. "Are you all right?"

"Yes."

"Would you like some coffee?"

"Yes, please."

Cullen poured her a cup from the tiny pot on the minibar and took it to her.

Esther was sitting by the window, her hair falling around her in a wild golden halo. Without makeup and wearing a cute teal tunic the bellhop had grabbed from the gift shop, she looked like a little girl.

Cullen handed her the steaming coffee and stepped back. He had to refrain from grabbing her up and hugging her close. If he understood one thing from all of her father's letters, it was that he must always respect Esther and treat her like the lady her father had told him she was. Cullen would never disrespect Esther by ogling her while she was still half-asleep.

But he still wanted to hold her and protect her.

"How are you?" he asked. He settled into a chair, unsure about all these feelings rushing like a river current through his mind.

"I didn't sleep much," she replied, her hands holding on to the mug. "I want to find the white rock."

"Then that's what we'll do."

She pointed to the papers scattered on the tiny desk. "I reorganized everything. All the underlined hints, all the passages with exclamation points, everything. I circled words and even underlined things as he'd written them."

She took a sip of coffee, her expression scattered and searching. Why did it seem as if she was holding back?

Telling himself he was imagining things, Cullen tapped his fingers on the chair. "I always looked forward to getting a letter from Jefferson Carlisle. In the world of email and texting and Twitter, well, it was nice to write back and forth the old-fashioned way."

He looked up at her then, his heart surfacing and opening. "At first, it was all about the diamond," he said. "But after a while, I wanted more information on you. I didn't want to admit it, but I don't think I can hide it anymore."

Esther sat with her knees up and her coffee in her hands, her gaze holding his, her eyes brightening to gold-and-yellow, then settling back to bronzed brown. She swallowed, sighed, held him there. "I have a confession to make, too."

Surprise and curiosity tore through Cullen. "Really, now? What's that, luv? You have the diamond and you've been holding out?"

She pushed at her hair and placed her near-empty cup on the table. "No, nothing like that." Then she pointed to the documents. "I found something in my father's desk the other day, but I haven't had a chance to tell you about it."

Cullen couldn't take this. He got up, paced around, wondered if she'd realized the whole truth. Had she found his last letter to her father, the one Cullen prayed she wouldn't find? "What?"

"Some of your letters to him. Only two or three, but I understand so much more now why you want that diamond."

The diamond. She still believed he wanted the diamond. He breathed in relief and regret in one gulp. He did want the diamond. Didn't he?

Swallowing, he tugged his hand down his face. "And what do you understand about me now?"

She got up, tied her heavy robe tight over her T-shirt, tied her smile tight, too. "How you grew up. How your father treated you. Why you want security for your mother and your sisters. You tried to explain, but I didn't listen."

He closed his eyes to the memories. "You know me so well from a couple of silly letters?"

"Those were not silly words," she said, reaching out to take his hand. "That was a man comfortable in his own skin telling a mentor why he's worked so hard to be a success. You told my father that you loved your family, that you missed your father even though you still hadn't quite forgiven him for all he put you through. You trusted my father with your deepest fears and your best hopes." She let go of his hand

and fell back on the chair. "I wish both of you had trusted me, too."

Cullen saw the pain and disappointment there in her eyes. "I'm so sorry—"

She stopped him with her hand raised. "I'm glad my father picked you, Cullen."

Unable to take the sweet need in her eyes, Cullen said, "You need to get dressed." Then he turned and went out the door, shutting it behind him.

But, oh, how he wanted to stay.

Now, why had she gone and told Cullen that? It was obvious that she'd upset him by reading his personal letters. But her father had left those letters there for a reason. And Cullen had brought her the other letters for a reason. She was beginning to suspect that reason wasn't necessarily all about finding some mystical diamond.

Maybe her father had set up this elaborate game, so *if* Cullen did come to her, she'd understand him more. And cut him some slack. Or maybe keep him near?

And she did understand him so much better now.

Esther went to the table and picked up one of the letters, the pages folded and crisp from being hidden away.

Dear Mr. Jefferson,
Your relationship with Esther sounds so special. I love
my mam and sisters, but I never got to know my father,
or rather, we lived in the same house but we were never
close. He died when I was in college. And because I
needed to provide for my family, I did some bad things.
I fell in with a man who had no scruples, but as long as
he paid me money, I was willing to be his lackey. I went
from bearing the brunt of my father's disappointments
and bitterness to being bonded to a man who would kill
me as soon as look at me. But I got away. I got out and

*the day I walked away I went into the nearest chapel
and I sat down and I prayed to be a better man.
    For my family.*

Esther stopped reading, the tears in her eyes misting like
the light rain outside in the Vieux Carré. For his family. Cullen did have honor. He was a noble man, after all.

He was fighting for integrity and dignity and hope.

And, he had turned back to God after he'd walked away
from evil.

But now that she had invaded his innermost thoughts, had
read his private admissions, would Cullen forgive her enough
to let her love him? To let God love him?

Or would he go after that diamond and never look back?

Cullen sat out on the sofa, staring at his travel bag. He still
had a few secrets left. But right now he felt raw and open and
completely out of breath.

Esther knew his pain. She'd seen it, heard it, in his words
to her dad. Did she pity him now? Did she imagine him as
the scared little boy and the gangly teenager who tried to
fight back?

No. He'd overcome all of that. He'd educated himself,
worked hard day and night to make a name for himself. People respected him. He'd made some important discoveries
that would go down in thc history books.

But maybe his most important discovery was in the next
room. He wished he could live up to her standards. He prayed
that he could tell her in person what he'd told her father in
that last letter. Where had Jefferson put that particular letter?

Cullen went to the window and stared out at the spires of
the St. Louis Cathedral, his heart hitting at his chest with a
new cadence. And for the first time since he'd sat in that chapel after walking away from Charles Hogan, Cullen prayed

in earnest to the God he'd been avoiding. He wanted God back in his life, because he wanted to keep Esther in his life.

Esther took a quick shower, then tossed on the comfortable black leggings and the teal tunic the concierge had sent up, and found her sandals. Grabbing a granola bar from the fully stocked hotel minibar, she opened the door and found Cullen checking his phone.

He looked up, smiled in appreciation even while his eyes avoided hers. "You clean up nicely."

Esther tossed her hair over her shoulder. "I forgot my hair clip. It's on the nightstand."

He finally glanced up and straight at her. "I like it down."

She left it down.

Wanting to distance herself a little bit for her own sanity, she nodded toward the phone. "Are you doing diamond research?"

"I have a few files stashed in here," he admitted. "I thought I might see a correlation between what I have and what your father sent." He put down the phone. "We never discussed seeing Mr. Reynolds in the park yesterday. Maybe we should have confronted him."

She sank down in a chair across from the couch. "He could have been strolling, getting exercise."

"In a thunderstorm?"

"He got caught by surprise."

"I'd say. In more ways than one."

Esther shook her head. "I can't picture sweet Mr. Reynolds as a thief or criminal."

"But he could have been the one who alerted Big Foot and Tiny Tim yesterday. I find it mighty convenient that he was nearby when Big Foot tried to take us out."

Esther got up, her hands on her hips. "Suppose Mr. Reynolds was simply an innocent witness."

"Then did he see us there?"

"I don't know, because you wouldn't let me talk to him. And, we left the scene before the police could interview us."

"We didn't give them our IDs, and Big Foot isn't going to talk, trust me."

"What if Mr. Reynolds did see us and told them that?"

"We'll worry about that when it happens," Cullen said. "Right now, I'd rather get to the immediate problem. We still have a missing diamond and we still have someone out there who wants to find it before we do."

Esther grabbed some coffee and washed down the rest of the granola bar. "So you never noticed any of this—the clues and hints—when you first read the letters?"

Cullen put away his phone. "No. I thought your father was eccentric. I only focused on what looked to be fact. And the facts showed me that the diamond was somewhere in this city or near New Orleans, maybe somewhere in the swamps. But after going back over my own notes, I did find a couple of things that might help. I've studied this thing to death, you know."

She smiled at that. "You are dedicated to finding that diamond."

He got up and came to her. Esther had to take in a breath at the force from his eyes. The way he looked at her scared her.

"What is it, Cullen?"

"I'm more dedicated to keeping you alive."

Then he pulled her close and kissed her, his warm hand holding her neck. Esther drew back, but she couldn't resist touching his tanned skin. She ran her fingers down his jawline.

"We can't go past finding the diamond right now. I won't allow it to fall into the wrong hands, and the only way to stop that is to find it. And after that…"

He brought her close, his hands now on her elbows. "After that, we might have a chance?"

Esther swallowed, closed her eyes. "After that, you'll probably be gone."

Cullen stepped away.

Maybe she had read his last letter to her father, after all.

NINETEEN

They had a plan.

Esther would put together the clues, while Cullen would research the people Esther and her father knew best—the Reynoldses and Ted and a few regulars in Esther's life—including Harold, the saxophone player. And he'd go back through his information channels and see what was going on with the infamous Charles Hogan.

So they worked all morning, quietly at times, and discussing back and forth at other times. And all the while, Cullen couldn't get Esther's earlier statement to him out of his mind.

After that, you'll probably be gone.

She knew him so well. And yet, she didn't know him at all. Because he wasn't so confident or sure anymore. And he wasn't so ready to be gone.

So he kept working toward the ultimate goal—laying claim to finding one of the rarest and most valuable jewels in the world.

Every now and then, he'd glance up at the woman sitting across from the desk and marvel at the intensity of her delicate features, of the way she lifted those dark eyebrows whenever she thought she was on to something, of the way she glanced up and right into his eyes, then quickly lowered her gaze.

Cullen made calls, secured internet sites and jotted down

coordinates and clues, his softening heart pounding a solid message into his hardheaded brain.

You're in love with Esther.

You're in love with Esther.

Dear Lord, what am I supposed to do? he prayed, his pleas silent inside his head.

What did he do? Honor his promise to her father, or honor his own selfish need for security and recognition? What did he do? Because he was pretty sure the precious jewel he now wanted had golden eyes and wore cute little cloglike sandals.

"I know what we need to do," Esther said, getting up to dance around the room.

Cullen caught his breath and enjoyed watching her. "What's that, luv?"

"I'm been looking for the wrong book," she said, her hands moving in animation. "It's not the Audubon bird book. It's another book Father gave me when I turned thirteen."

"And where is this book?"

"It's at the shop—in the apartment upstairs. I put it up there after he died."

Cullen sat up, waiting. "And what's the book about?"

"The White Rock Chapel." She smiled a sweet smile. "It's a book about a princess who lives in the swamp with her falcon and her egrets, and she meets an adventurer, a pirate of sorts." She stopped, stared at Cullen, then shook her head. "He hunts and traps and he's larger than life, but he is a Louisiana character, with our local traditions in every aspect of his life. He has two white tigers. He teaches the princess about hunting and she teaches him to respect the land and save the innocent animals. Father used to tell me the book was a metaphor for the pure earth and the need for humans to use it wisely."

She paced a little, then tapped her notes. "So after I put things together with the falcon, the tigers and the way my father always called me a princess when I wore my white dress, I thought about the white rock and why that sounded so familiar. And that's it. There's a book, but the name is in French. Life at White Rock Chapel—*Vie à la Chapelle Blanche de Roche*."

"Okay, so what does that have to do with the chocolate diamond?"

She sank down on the couch again. "I think the White Rock Chapel is a real place, Cullen. I believe I've been there, once when I was very small. I think I can find my way back."

She stood, stretched and then leaned down. "I think that's where we'll find the Levi-Lafitte Diamond."

"Do we need the book first?"

"Yes," she said. "We have to find the book so I can match the details."

"Let's go, then."

They bought hats from a souvenirs shop. Esther hid her hair underneath her big straw hat and donned a pair of huge dark designer-knockoff shades while Cullen wore a new fedora and a cool pair of aviator sunglasses. The concierge had sent their wet clothes out to the cleaners yesterday and had delivered them back in time for them to change again, with new shirts over their clean jeans.

"Do we look like tourists?" Esther asked, excitement coloring her tone.

"You look like the loveliest tourist I've ever met," Cullen replied. "Maybe a mysterious movie star out for a stroll on the Moonwalk."

"Yes, Angelina Jolie, eat your heart out."

He lowered his shades. "And how do I look?"

"Better than Brad Pitt, let me tell you."

He shot her a devastating smile. "Maybe we'll draw too much attention, as stunning as we are."

Esther glanced around. "I'm beginning to confuse who's a tourist and who's a criminal."

"Just pretend you don't have a care in the world."

"If only that were true."

"We can try at least. Starting now."

He pulled her into his arms and gave her a kiss. "See, we're happy, carefree, mad about each other."

Esther's heart seemed to like that idea. "Well, I am mad *at* you most of the time."

"Not quite what I had in mind."

She wanted to tell him that if he kissed her again, she'd forgive him. But Esther still couldn't let go of the image of him walking away. She knew in her heart he would, as surely as she knew he'd promised her he wouldn't. Some promises were too hard to keep. He was a good man, deep underneath that adventurer's need to be first. But she wanted him to make her first in his heart. And he couldn't do that.

She saw their conflict, front and center.

She was where she wanted to be. Maybe not free to roam or choose, but she owed it to her father to keep Carlisle Collectibles going.

Cullen was where he didn't really want to be. He was a traveler passing through. He couldn't settle down and he wouldn't settle for her. He wanted that diamond, and Esther didn't think any pact or pledge he'd made under duress would keep him from taking it.

So she accepted that and went on with their mission.

What else could she do?

Would she ever be safe again? Would she ever love again?

Love. She was in love with Cullen.

Dear Lord, why did this happen? Why did I let this happen?

Her prayers went from surprise to acceptance to resolve.

Lord, help me to get through this and move on with my life. Help me to accept, to appreciate, to live.

Really live.

She saw it now as they strolled through the city she loved.

In the months since her father's death, she hadn't really been living at all. She'd only been putting one foot in front of the other, trying to live up to what her deceased parents expected, trying to bury her guilt in gilded treasures and sentimental things. No wonder she didn't have a clue about the diamond or all the people who wanted it so badly. She'd shut herself off from feeling, from noticing things that used to bring her joy. She was like that princess in the white dress—alone in the forest—only, the dress Esther had chosen was too big, too aged and too heavy with memories for her to ever fit into it.

Had she been waiting for a prince?

Or had she been waiting to come alive again?

Esther wanted to feel this way even after Cullen was gone.

She had to live her life—for herself. For God. Her parents would want that. And she could do that now, thanks to this time with Cullen, thanks to her father's letters and his gift of this one last adventure.

Needing to keep her mind off this newest revelation, she whispered to Cullen. "What did your background checks reveal?"

He smiled down at her, held her hand, pointed to a riverboat out on the Mississippi as if he didn't have a care in the world. "The Reynoldses are clean. No worries there as far as I could find, not even a traffic violation. Your Ted had some issues when he was younger—arrests for petty thief and truancy, but you sort of knew that anyway. And the saxophone player—a lonely street musician who served in the army and now has post-traumatic stress issues. He doesn't want to live in a shelter so he plays for tips and rents a room up on Anna Street."

"And Charles Hogan?"

"Still out of the country, supposedly. I can't seem to get a thread on where the man is right now."

"But we can't be sure that he's out of the country."

"No. We can never really be sure of anything."

That comment hit home. She'd never really be sure of him.

"So right now, we're still in the same spot."

Cullen nuzzled her hair. "Yes. We get in, find that book and go from there."

They crossed Decatur and cut through Jackson Square. The grounds were crowded with artists, musicians, tarot card readers and vendors selling their wares, along with tourists from all over the world.

Cullen held her hand and glanced over at her. "When this is all over, I'd truly like to come back here and enjoy the beauty of New Orleans. With you."

Esther's heart lifted out over the now-blue late-afternoon sky. The air was humid with moisture, but her eyes were moist with tiny tears of joy and frustration. She wanted to ask if he would ever come back, but she wasn't sure she wanted to force him into telling her the truth.

They strolled along, then came out in front of the St. Louis Cathedral and headed toward Royal. Esther wanted to run the rest of the way, but she held herself back.

Finally, they made it to the shop's back courtyard. "Everything looks locked up tight," she said. Esther twisted the new lock open. "No signs of anyone trying to break in."

"They probably know your place is being watched. And since one of their men is in custody, maybe they think this shop is too hot right now."

"Let's hope so."

She pushed at the squeaky door. The shop smelled musty. Esther turned on lights and glanced up the aisles. An eerie silence greeted her. Some of the clocks had probably wound down and she'd have to go around and reset them. "Everything looks the same."

Cullen guided her up to the apartment. "Where did you last see the book?"

"On the desk," she said, hurrying toward the back room.

Cullen followed, looking here and there. "I don't think anyone's been back since we were last here."

Esther shuffled papers. "I didn't find anything substantial in what was locked inside the desk." She glanced over at Cullen. "Except those two letters from you, of course."

Cullen looked away and continued searching.

While Esther wondered what he'd had to say in all the other letters he sent to her father.

After going through old newspapers and magazines, tossing a few stacks of junk mail and saving what seemed important, Esther was about to give up. Then she saw the basket where her father always placed shipment orders. She started digging through the orders and hit on something solid.

"I found it!"

Cullen dropped the stack of trade magazines he'd been sorting through. "Are you sure?"

Esther held up the little battered book. "Yes." She pointed to the title. *"Vie à la Chapelle Blanche de Roche."*

"But where is this place?" Cullen asked. He pulled out his phone and did a quick search. "I found a White Rock Chapel in…Jean Lafitte, Louisiana. Jefferson Parish." He shook his head. "Coincidence?"

"Another of my father's little games. Jean Lafitte and Jefferson? It's practically telling us we're on the right track."

"Your father was an interesting man."

She rubbed a hand over the little children's book. "Yes, he was. This is so like him. And this has to be it."

She took his hand in hers. "It's a little church near the Intracoastal Waterway."

Cullen followed her down the stairs. "A town named after Jean Lafitte? Seriously."

"Yes. You know, he and his men were pardoned during the War of 1812 for helping General Andrew Jackson during the Battle of New Orleans."

"I remember that from my research." Cullen locked the door and they hurried away.

"We need my car," Esther said. "Let's go get it."

They turned from the gate toward the street.

And found a gun pointed at them.

"You're not going anywhere without me."

Mr. Reynolds.

"I'm going, too, sweetheart."

Mrs. Reynolds.

Esther glanced at the gun, then back at Cullen, shock rocking through her. "I thought they were clean."

"So did I. Obviously they never had a traffic violation, but they've been naughty nonetheless."

"I'll take your travel pouch, Mr. Murphy." Mrs. Reynolds's smile was puffy but deadly, the rouge on her cheeks cracking her wrinkles as she rummaged through Cullen's backpack. "Found the Remington, sweetie. No other weapons." She held the antique gun. "We have a car waiting. You two are going to take us to that diamond."

TWENTY

"You're kidding," Esther said in a loud voice as the SUV with dark-tinted windows left the city and headed south. "I mean, they're a nice old couple. She used to bake cookies for me." She shot a glance at the woman sitting beside her in the backseat.

"Shut up," Mrs. Reynolds said, a dainty pistol poking Esther in the ribs. Her smile was as sweet as ever, but her brown eyes held a desperate sparkle.

Mr. Reynolds sat up front with a gun on Cullen while Cullen drove. "Don't take it personally, dear. We want to retire and move to Miami."

Cullen glanced at Esther in the rearview mirror. "They want the money, Esther. But then, don't we all."

"I don't," Esther said. "I can't believe people I've trusted all of my life would stoop to this."

Mrs. Reynolds smiled that creepy painted smile, her gold earrings sparkling in the creamy dusk. "We didn't even know there was a diamond until—"

"We don't need to bore Esther with the details." Her husband sent her a warning scowl. "Let's get to this so-called chapel."

But Esther wanted details. "How did you figure it out?"

Mr. Reynolds stared at her from the front seat. "Someone told us you'd been searching through your children's books."

"Who?"

"Doesn't matter. We racked our brains but couldn't come up with anything. So we waited until you showed back up. Didn't work the other morning. Your friend here surprised both of us."

Cullen hit the steering wheel. "I knew it. I told you I didn't like him. Esther, he has my gun."

Esther felt sick to her stomach. The Reynoldses had sent the thugs after them.

"I don't like you either, young man. I've heard about you." Mr. Reynolds exhaled, then pointed the gun at Cullen. "I saw some of your notes that day in the upstairs apartment, Esther. And the word *white* stood out."

Mrs. Reynolds got excited, her hands flailing in the air. "I figured it out. I always thought the White Rock Chapel sounded so romantic. And you were holding the book today when we showed up."

"Did you hire those two men who broke into my shop?"

"Oh, my. I don't condone killing," the old woman replied, clearly upset and confused. "Raymond, tell them. They weren't supposed to shoot you."

Her husband shrugged. "We don't have to deal with that. We've done our part."

"Which is?" Cullen asked, his gaze holding Esther's.

"Nothing. Drive."

Cullen cut his gaze toward the other man. "You get a cut if you deliver us to someone else?"

"Yes," Helen Reynolds said with a smile. "A nice little nest egg."

"Bea, shut up!"

The SUV grew quiet and then Mr. Reynolds sat up straight. "Turn here."

An hour or so out from New Orleans, Cullen pulled the SUV off a deserted road near the Intracoastal Waterway. The sun was going down to the west, its rays clinging to the dusk in shades of gold, amber and pink.

There amid palmetto palms and twisted, aged mossy oaks, sat a tiny whitewashed stone chapel with a hand-carved sign over the door that read *Vie à la Chapelle Blanche de Roche*.

"An old amusement park," Cullen said, glancing around. Some sort of putt-putt golf place complete with a miniature Mayan ruins and an overgrown jungle with fake birds sitting everywhere. And a mural of two white tigers painted across an old fence. Rex and Zulu.

"The White Rock Chapel," Esther said on a whisper. "I do remember this place. He brought me here once, when I was very young." She shook her head. "All the clues are here. This place had a snake exhibit and a bird aviary with a white falcon. It had little rivers named after famous real rivers. It's full of folklore and faith. The chapel was at the center. It was the final hole in the putt-putt golf game."

"They were married here, dear," Mrs. Reynolds said, her words so full of compassion Esther forgot the woman had a gun on her. "They thought the little chapel in the middle of this fun place was perfect."

"He never told me that."

"He never told you a lot of things," Mr. Reynolds said. "Let's go inside."

Esther glanced at Cullen. What were they going to do now? She knew what she wanted to do. Grab these weapons from the senior-citizen brigade and find that diamond. But this place was far from town, with a bayou on one side and big water on the other. That diamond could be anywhere. And they could be dead by nightfall.

Cullen waited for Esther and Mrs. Reynolds, then stepped up onto the tiny porch. "A rather small church, don't you think?"

"People down here take such things very seriously," Mr.

Reynolds retorted with a smirk. "They still come here to pray and to get married, hold christenings, such silly things."

"You don't believe?" Cullen asked, his eyes holding Esther, willing her not to try anything rash. But his lovely Esther had *reckless* written all over her pretty face. He had to think of something quick.

"No, I don't believe," Mr. Reynolds shot back. "I only believe in cold, hard cash and that's what I've been promised. Now get inside so I can get my payoff and leave."

"Who's paying you?"

"We can't say," Mrs. Reynolds replied, her lips twisted upward.

Cullen had a sneaking suspicion he knew the answer anyway.

He opened the dark wooden door and entered the candlelit chapel. It was small, maybe ten feet wide and fifteen feet long, but it was clean and polished. A small altar was centered in front of a round stained-glass depiction of the Lord's Supper. It was hard to see in the dim light, but a small cross sat on the altar.

Mr. Reynolds pushed Cullen down onto one of the white pews. "Sit. They should be here soon."

Esther slid in beside Cullen and sent him a covert glance. "I thought this place was like a child's playhouse. I didn't realize how special it was to my parents."

The Reynoldses paced back and forth. Cullen leaned in. "I think I can take him. What about her?"

Esther gave a discreet lifting of her chin. "I can handle her."

"Don't get yourself shot. Distract her."

"Stop whispering," Mr. Reynolds said, his pistol waving.

Esther glanced up at him. "We were praying."

Cullen knew Esther had been praying. He'd said a few himself. *Protect her, Lord. She's the only one who is innocent in all of this.*

"It's always a good idea to pray, if you believe in that sort of thing," Mrs. Reynolds said. The woman seemed jittery and confused. Her gaze kept darting toward the door off to the side of the altar. "Raymond, they're late."

"They'll be here, Helen."

"I don't like this," she said on a whine.

"I don't like your nagging, but I have to listen to it every day."

And they were off and running, arguing back and forth about what they should do.

Cullen looked at Esther. Oh, yeah, they could take these two. "Distraction," he whispered, indicating Mrs. Reynolds.

Esther stood up. "Uh, Mrs. Reynolds, how did you know my parents got married here?"

Helen stopped in midsentence. "Your father told me the day he brought you here on your eighth birthday. The park was closing for good, but the locals wanted to keep the chapel. He said he wanted you to see this spot and remember how much they both loved you." She sent Esther a saccharine smile.

Esther inched close to the pacing woman. "This is such a lovely place."

Cullen couldn't argue with that. The setting sun cut glittering rays through the stained-glass windows, casting a bright light on the front of the church.

He watched Esther. She looked around at the walls, then glanced back to the altar.

And gasped.

Cullen turned for a brief second. "Esther?"

"I'm okay," she said, holding a hand to her head. "I feel faint. I haven't eaten all day."

"We didn't bring any food." Helen glared at her husband. "Because, as usual, someone didn't plan ahead."

"Helen, I'm doing the best I can," Mr. Reynolds shouted, his hands going up in the air. "I do wish they'd hurry up."

They slung words at each other while Esther stared at the altar. Cullen followed her gaze and almost gasped himself. There on the tiny altar was the cross he'd noticed before, only now it was shimmering in the evening sun. The cross, forged from iron, stood about a foot tall on a wooden pedestal. And embedded in the heavy steel was a beautiful Victorian clock face surrounded by intricate gold filigree, with a doorknob inside the clock. A doorknob with a rich golden-brown jeweled center.

Cullen looked at Esther, his heart pumping. She tilted her head and rushed between the Reynoldses. "Mrs. Reynolds, I think I'm going to—"

Esther dropped to the polished wooden floor.

Mrs. Reynolds screamed and dropped down beside her.

"She's ill." Cullen went on a knee, then turned to Mr. Reynolds, giving the old man time to forget he had a gun.

Cullen swooped up and around and knocked hard on Mr. Reynold's fleshy wrist, causing him to drop the gun.

Esther pushed at Mrs. Reynolds, knocking her off her chunky feet, then held her down with one hand while she yanked the pistol away with her other hand. "I've got her," she shouted to Cullen.

Cullen caught the other gun by the barrel and reeled it in, his hand griping Mr. Reynold's arm. He lifted Mr. Reynolds up and onto the pew. Esther did the same with Helen.

"Who hired you?" Cullen asked.

Esther stood watching the doors, her gaze swaying back toward that cross and Cullen.

Cullen knew two things about that altarpiece.

Esther had designed the cross.

And the doorknob she'd put in the center held the Levi-Lafitte Diamond.

"Who hired you?" he asked again. Did the couple even know they were sitting less than five feet away from the diamond? Probably not.

"We can't tell," Helen said, sniffing back tears. "They told us they'd kill us. We were told to get you here and then they'd make you tell where the diamond is."

"He came to me, offered me a lot of money," Mr. Reynolds said. "We wanted to be closer to our grandchildren."

"So you went after Esther to make that happen?"

"They only wanted to scare you," the man explained. "So you'd either leave or tell someone about the diamond."

"I don't know about the diamond," Esther said. "All you had to do was ask, but then you wouldn't get rich, would you?"

"It's hard times, Esther," Mrs. Reynolds said, her sobs growing louder. "Hard times."

Esther leaned in, her gaze steely. "Did you help murder my father?"

"What are you talking about?"

Cullen wanted answers, but they needed to grab that diamond and leave before the others arrived. "Esther, we need to go." He gave her a warning look. "Now."

"But—" She looked toward the altar.

"We're taking you back to New Orleans," Cullen said. "To the police."

"No. We can't leave until—"

The back door opened and Ted walked in, his sprained ankle apparently healed. "Nobody's leaving until I say so." He had a gun trained on Cullen. "Now, Mr. Murphy, put down that weapon. Esther, hand your gun back to Mrs. Reynolds. Then both of you find a seat. We're not leaving until you tell me where that diamond is hidden."

Cullen did as he asked, and prayed Esther would do the same. Now that everyone seemed to be here, maybe he could finally get her and the diamond out of here. But how?

The Reynolds team took back their weapons and stood next to Ted. "We didn't get to that part yet."

"That's not your part," Ted said on a grin. "You know that, Raymond."

"Then I want my money so I can leave."

"Stop whining," Ted said, rolling his eyes.

"Ted, why are you doing this?" Esther asked, shock coloring her flushed face. "What's going on?"

Ted's chuckle settled into a smirk. "What's going on? I worked myself to the bone in that dusty old shop and all that time I've had to listen to the stories about that big diamond. Well, I wanted to find the thing, not listen to your daddy spin tales about it. So I started taking notes when your father would go into one of his rambling speculations. I almost had him convinced to put out a search party." He shot a hostile look toward Cullen. "Then *he* got involved and Jefferson quit talking to me about it. Wouldn't tell me a thing. Nothing, Esther. Not a thing."

Cullen grunted. "So you want in on the cut, too."

"He's in," Mrs. Reynolds said. "He's getting more than we are."

"Shut up," her husband said on a hiss.

"Someone is paying you, too?" Esther asked, her frown filled with anger. "Is there anyone around here I can really trust?"

"Me," Cullen reminded her. "You can trust me."

"Yeah, right," Ted said, snorting a laugh. "He didn't tell you everything, did he?"

Esther searched Cullen's face. "What's he talking about?"

"I have no idea," Cullen said, dread trickling down his backbone.

"Let me fill you in," Ted said. "I found some of his letters to your father. Touching, really. And full of personal details. A regular confession." Ted pushed Cullen back against the pew. "Relax. I'll tell you both everything."

Esther stood up. "Cullen told me that diamond could bring out the worst in people. Now I believe him."

"Well, believe this, too," Ted said, circling, his gun at the ready. "Your Irish friend admitted he used to be a diamond thief. And now, he's back for one more heist, because he's the one who hid it around here somewhere, only your daddy found it and hid it again. But I don't suppose either of them shared that little tidbit with you, did they?"

TWENTY-ONE

Esther's gaze filled with hurt and bewilderment, but her eyes never left Cullen. "You knew where the diamond was all this time?

Cullen couldn't deny the truth. He hated the hurt in her eyes, hated the snicker he heard coming from Ted Dunbar. Hated the man he used to be.

He shook his head. "No. Not exactly. I knew the diamond was in Louisiana because I did find it while I was here. I didn't give it to Hogan, however. Hogan owns property near New Orleans, remember, and I was afraid once he discovered the truth, he might find the real diamond before I did. That's why I came back."

"He came back to steal the diamond away from you, Esther," Ted said, his tone smug. "He's been playing you."

Esther focused on Cullen. "You've been here before, to this chapel?"

"No." He sank down, weary with all the deceit. "I stayed at Hogan's house once when I still worked for him—a long time ago. He wanted me to search for the diamond. He bought the property because he believed the diamond was located on the grounds somewhere." He shrugged. "Based on what I'd researched and some old maps he'd found when he bought his estate, I established a timeline and I went out alone and searched without his knowledge. I found the diamond, buried in a box underneath an old oak on one of the Indian mounds near the bayou. But I didn't tell Hogan I'd found it. It became my insurance policy."

"But you got away," she said. "You told me you got away."

"He did get away," Ted said, leaning down over Esther. "He had already found a smaller diamond in Australia very much like our beloved Levi-Lafitte Diamond. He had it shipped here and handed that one over to Charles Hogan."

"The fake one?" Esther shook her head. "You told me about that. How he's figured out it wasn't the real one."

Ted started to speak, but Cullen stood and grabbed him by the collar. "Shoot me if you want, but I'll speak for myself first, understand?"

"Go for it, man," Ted said, his bravado diminished. "This ought to be good."

Cullen sat down beside Esther. "I gave him the other one and for years, he believed it was real. He couldn't admit to anyone he had the diamond, so he had to be careful about having it appraised. But the real one—"

"The real one hadn't been found. Isn't that why we're here?"

Ted looked disappointed. "You didn't believe him, did you, Esther?"

"Of course I believed him," she said, tears forming in her eyes. "But I believed you, too, Ted." She pointed to the Reynoldses. "And I believed them. I wanted to believe my father, but he couldn't even tell me the truth. Right now, I don't trust any of you. I don't believe anything."

Cullen's heart felt as hard as a diamond, but it also seemed to be shattering into a million pieces. Esther's pain hit at him like sharp shards of crystal.

"I hid the real one, Esther. I never told anyone I had it. I let Charles Hogan believe he had the real thing, to protect my family."

"And so you could live the high life," Ted said, sneering at him. "I've checked you out, Murphy. You're not a pauper."

"No, I'm not. But I earned everything I own. I never sold the real Levi-Lafitte Diamond. I gave it to someone here in Louisiana for safekeeping. I made him promise to hide the diamond, even from me."

Esther put a hand to her mouth. "My father? You gave it to my father?"

"Yes," Cullen said. "And he hid it well."

Esther couldn't understand what she'd heard. It didn't make a bit of sense. And she was supposed to trust him? How could she ever trust any of them again?

"Ted, did you know this?"

Ted had gone pale. "No. No, I thought Cullen was playing *you*." He glared over at Mr. Reynolds. "I think Jefferson Carlisle did a number on all of us."

"Is Hogan behind this?" Cullen asked, staring up at Ted. "Is he?"

"I'm not talking," Ted said. But he looked at the door, his face twisted in a nervous tic.

Esther understood now. "So that's why you started corresponding with my father? You wanted someone you could trust to keep it safe? But why him? Why not hide it somewhere in Ireland?"

Cullen shrugged. "I thought it would be safer here. Too many hands passing it around could be dangerous. We talked, sometimes on the phone, but mostly with those letters. We conceived a plan to protect the diamond until I could get here. It was his idea to 'speculate' about the diamond in his letters, to throw off anyone who might get suspicious."

"Useless ramblings," Ted said, kicking at the step behind him. He held the gun to Cullen's head. "If you know where that diamond is, you'd better tell me now."

"I don't," Cullen said, giving Esther a warning look. "Mr.

Carlisle hid it so well, I couldn't find it. And he died before he could tell me anything." He turned on Ted. "Or maybe I should say, someone poisoned him before he could say anything. If he had lived, we wouldn't be sitting here now."

Ted shook his head. "Don't look at me, man. It was their idea to up his heart medication so we could search the shop for the diamond."

Esther shot up off the pew. "You all killed him." She pointed at Cullen. "You, with your grand scheme to hide the diamond—you got him involved by taking advantage of his obsession. And you, Ted, how could you do that to him, knowing how much he loved you?" She walked over to the Reynoldses. "Do you know how much I miss my father? And you killed him for money?"

She gulped in a sob. Cullen rushed to her, but she pushed him away. "Don't touch me. Don't ever come near me again."

"Esther—"

She held up a hand in warning. "No."

They'd all lied to her, used her and Cullen had allowed her life to be ruined so he could find that diamond again. "You could have told me the truth that first day," she said, staring up at him. "But you let me go on and on. You let me read those letters."

"I tried to find a way to tell you," Cullen said. "I...I didn't know how to explain it. I didn't know where he'd hidden the diamond."

"We still don't know that," Ted replied. "I thought we'd find it in the swamp around this place."

"Well, I know." She pushed past Cullen, determined to end this now. "You all want the diamond? Is that it?"

"Esther!" She heard Cullen's voice, felt his hand brush her arm. "Esther, don't."

But she was beyond listening. "I know exactly where the Levi-Lafitte Diamond is. My father left those clues for me and me alone."

She pointed to the altar. "It's right there where it's been all along. I made this sculpture a few years ago with a clock face and one of my father's precious doorknobs. Only, he told me it was cheap glass." She picked up the heavy cross and brought it down the steps. "I didn't even notice the diamond. I thought I was working with a piece of costume jewelry."

Ted stepped forward, his mouth gaping open. "You're kidding, right?"

Mr. Reynolds pulled a loupe out of his pocket. "Let me see, Esther."

They all followed her and stood silent while Mr. Reynolds examined the big chunk of what looked like rich chocolate glass.

"I do believe it's the real deal this time," he said, grinning. "Esther, you found it. You found the Levi-Lafitte Diamond."

She looked at Cullen. "Yes, I did. And now I'm going home. I don't care if the rest of you fight over it, or shoot each other over it. I want to go back to my life."

"Esther?"

She heard Cullen, but she kept on walking. She had to get out of here. But when she reached the door, an older man stepped into the room. He had crisp gray hair and wore a lightweight khaki shirt and cargo pants. "Hello, Esther."

Esther heard Cullen's hiss of breath behind her.

"Charles Hogan?" she asked, not even surprised.

"Yes, my dear." He glanced around her. "And I see the gang's all here."

Esther glanced back, saw the look of regret and longing on Cullen's face. "Yes," she said, biting back tears. "And they're all yours. You finally have your treasure."

She tried to move past him, but he grabbed her arm. "Not so fast, young lady."

Then he whirled her around and held a knife to her throat. "You're as much as part of this as they are, I'm afraid."

* * *

"Let her go," Cullen said, his mind churning. He could grab a gun and try to shoot Hogan, but Esther might get hit.

Hogan read his mind. "Reynolds, gather the weapons and bring them to me."

Mr. Reynolds did as he asked while his wife whimpered and sobbed.

Cullen's worst nightmare had come true. Why had he gotten Esther involved in this? He could have searched for the diamond without her.

But you made a pledge to her father. A promise to protect her. A promise that he'd choose Esther over all else—even the diamond.

Cullen hadn't really taken that pledge seriously until he'd met Esther and fallen in love with her. Now he'd caught her up in the web of lies he'd been trying to untangle.

Hogan eyed the sculpture. "Ted, be a dove and bring me that, please."

Ted's eyes bulged. "Not until I get my cut."

Hogan yanked Esther close, then pressed the knife against her skin. "If you don't do as I say, she'll get the first cut. Set it there by the door."

Ted placed it near Hogan's feet.

Hogan let out a chuckle after Ted hurriedly got out of his way. "Ted, my dear boy, you didn't deliver the diamond to me. I had to come here myself and what do I find? One of my men cowering in jail, another sneaking out of the country and you three imbeciles standing here arguing, when the diamond was right there for the taking."

Ted shivered and twitched. "We got Esther and the Irishman here."

"Enough!" Hogan shouted, edging the knife closer to Esther. "If you don't shut up, I will kill her."

Mrs. Reynolds sobbed into her hand while her husband's breathing grew more erratic. Ted turned a pale white.

And Esther stared straight ahead, a grim resolve on her face.

Cullen couldn't stand this. "Hogan, let Esther go. Take me and the diamond. We'll be even then."

"Oh, we'll never be even," Hogan replied, his arm tightening against Esther. "I don't forgive people who trick me and lie to me. I gave you a job," Hogan said. "I saved you from poverty and despair. And this is the thanks I get?"

"You made me your slave," Cullen retorted. "I broke free and you've never forgotten."

"You're right about that," Hogan said. "I do not stand for being tricked and mocked." He glanced down at the sculpture. "An interesting piece. A real treasure." He whirled Esther around, the knife shining like liquid silver in the dim lighting. "Pick that up for me, young lady."

Esther lifted the heavy cross and held it with both hands.

"Now you have to suffer, Murphy. You have two choices— the diamond or the girl. It's your call."

Cullen knew the answer to that. "Let Esther go."

Hogan laughed again. "So you want the girl, huh? Well, well. You have become soft." He nudged Esther. "I lied. I'm taking both of your treasures."

"Don't do this," Cullen said, inching closer. "You can have the diamond."

Ted moved closer. "Don't hurt her."

"You're quite popular, my darling," Hogan said in Esther's ear. "But you can't stay here with your admirers any longer."

Esther didn't protest. She held herself rigid, like a queen about to be executed. But Cullen knew if Hogan took her, it would be a death sentence.

Before Cullen could make a move, Ted ran forward. "Take her. I don't care. But I want my cut from this rock. I want out of New Orleans."

Hogan stared at Ted, surprise warring with anger in his

expression. He moved toward the door with Esther. "I'll keep that in mind."

Cullen shot forward and grabbed one of the guns from the pile on the pew, then started after Hogan.

"Stop," the man said, whirling around again. He pressed the knife blade to Esther's throat, drawing blood. "Drop the weapon, Murphy."

Cullen saw the terror in Esther's eyes. He placed the gun on the floor.

Hogan leaned close to Esther. "Hold tight and we'll be out of here soon."

"Let her go," Cullen said. "Please. This is between you and me, Hogan. Let's end it here."

"It will never end," Hogan said. "I have to make you pay." He brushed the knife down Esther's hair. "And now I think I've finally found a way."

Esther held tight to the sculpture, her eyes wide.

"Esther, I love you," Cullen said. "Esther?"

But Esther wasn't listening.

TWENTY-TWO

"Open the door." Hogan pushed Esther toward the big truck.

The minute Hogan lifted the knife away, Esther twisted and rammed the sculpture base into the man's throat and then hit him with the big door. Caught by surprise, Hogan lashed out with the knife, but Esther was free now.

"Run, Esther!" Cullen fired at Hogan, but missed.

Esther ran away but turned once, her eyes meeting Cullen's. "You have what you came for. So leave." Then she tossed the sculpture toward him and took off.

"Esther!"

She ran into the darkness.

Ted burst out the door, now armed with his own weapon—Cullen's Remington pistol. Hogan got up, stumbled toward them but before Cullen could raise his weapon, Ted fired once, twice. And seemed shocked that the old gun actually worked.

Hogan went down and didn't move.

Cullen ran into the swampy woods. "Esther, it's over. You're safe now."

She didn't answer.

He heard tires squealing and rushed back toward the vehicles. And watched as the SUV took off down the dirt road.

Esther was gone.

Cullen looked around at Ted. Ted had the sculpture, holding it close. "I'm not giving it to you," he said.

"Yes, you are." Cullen walked toward him, daring him to fire again. "You will give me that cross or I'll shoot you where you stand." He raised his gun, waiting for Ted to do the same.

Ted started whimpering and held the sculpture out to Cullen. "I want my cut."

"You chose this over Esther. You got what you deserved."

"Yeah, well, what about you?"

"You don't know a thing about me."

Cullen got in Hogan's truck, but rolled down the window. "I'm going to the closest police station to report everything. You and your friends might want to either start walking, or hide out in the swamp."

"Hey," Ted called, running after the truck. "Hey, you hurt her more than I did, man."

"You're right," Cullen said. "But I'm going to make that up to her."

One month later

Fall had come to the Quarter. The air was less humid, the tourists less fussy and aggressive. The streets not as loud.

Quiet.

That's what Esther craved. Complete quiet.

But when the quiet finally came at the end of each day, she only felt alone and lost.

Ted was gone, arrested along with the Reynoldses for premeditated murder, aggravated kidnapping and various other criminal activities stemming from their association with Charles Hogan.

Esther hadn't gotten around to hiring a new assistant, but she had put a Going Out of Business sign on the door and she was selling off most of her inventory for below-market prices.

She'd given the police her statement and told the truth

about everything. She'd even told them about Cullen. Technically, he'd done nothing wrong. He hadn't kidnapped her, or harassed her, and he hadn't broken into her property.

But, he had broken her heart. Only there wasn't a law against that. Besides, she figured he had friends in high places. He'd give a statement and he'd be cleared.

No one really cared about the missing diamond.

Because no one believed there was a real diamond.

And Esther would neither confirm nor deny that. Cullen had taken the diamond. He'd accomplished his mission.

Esther was going on with her life.

She was going to travel and take notes and study her art. She was going to create vivid pieces out of all the graven images she'd seen and studied all of her life. She'd use the bottled-up emotions churning through her system to help.

And she was going to try to forget Cullen Murphy.

She looked at one of the few remaining clocks and saw it was time to lock up. She hadn't noticed because she hadn't heard the saxophone player. Where was her friend today, anyway?

Esther hurried to the door, intent on calling it a day.

But a hand touched on the wood, blocking her.

For a minute, her heart seemed to come alive again.

But when she looked up at the man standing there, a deep disappointment hit her and pushed her back.

"Harold? How are you?"

The saxophone player smiled at her. "I'm good, Miss Esther. I have to give you something."

Esther took the gold envelope. "What's this?"

"I don't know," the gaunt man replied. "This man gave me fifty bucks to deliver it to you."

Esther didn't want to hope, didn't want to believe, but...

"Who is this man?"

"I don't know that, either. But he said he'd be waiting at

the café if…if you want to talk." Harold turned to leave, then whirled back around. "Oh, and he said to read everything in that package."

Esther's hands shook. She locked the shop, then sat down in the office to open the envelope.
One folded letter, several pages thick, fell out.

Dear Esther:
I did lie to you. I didn't tell you why I went along with your father's elaborate plan instead of searching for the diamond myself. That's because I couldn't get up the nerve to admit to you that I was as fascinated by you as I was by this diamond.

You see, I looked forward to your father's letters more and more once he started telling me about you. He had the diamond and I believed it was safe, so I played along with his fun and games. And I wanted to meet you. I wanted to see the woman who had such a loyal father, a father who loved her and wanted only the best for her so much that he'd made me promise him I'd be there when she needed me. He trusted me, I think, because I was honest with him.

I first contacted your father because I had seen his article regarding the Levi-Lafitte Diamond. I was intrigued and wondered what his assumptions and research might yield. I decided after corresponding with him, he'd be the perfect person to protect the diamond. So I arranged to meet him and make the exchange. This was when you were in college.

But your father was paranoid so he came up with this scheme to throw people off. He would hide the diamond and not tell me where it was until I was ready to claim it. He'd write me a lot of rambling letters with a few clues thrown in. Now I know that Ted started watching and reading your father's mail. He also read my letters and I think he destroyed a lot of them. But your father was smart. He managed to sneak me one last letter right before he died. And he made me promise to never show that letter to anyone but you. I've enclosed that letter, so you will finally know the truth.

Esther saw her father's handwriting. She took a deep breath and read on:

Dear Cullen,
I don't have much time. I'm dying. I can't say much here but it won't be a __natural__ death. Just keep the letters I've sent and find Esther. She will figure this out. She will put together the clues I've left. You have to protect her, though. I think someone knows our secret. Protect my daughter, but let her help. She will do the right thing.

I want you and Esther to find the diamond. I owe her that much. She heard me fantasizing about it even when I knew where it was all along. I can't tell you where it is. I can't call you or see you. Too dangerous.

If anything happens to me, make sure Esther reads and analyzes the letters. She will figure this out and you can find the diamond based on my clues.

But, Cullen, you have to promise me one thing. You will take care of Esther. I know you and you are a good man. You will honor this request and you will be the best man for my Esther. I'm asking you to do this for me. And this is the most important part—choose Esther over the diamond. No matter what. You won't regret this.

And one last request, tell Esther I never regretted a minute of our life. Never. She is my proudest accomplishment. More precious than rubies or gold. Or even the diamond.

Esther's tears splashed on the black ink, smearing a few words. So many secrets, so much trouble for a diamond he knew he could never claim. Her father had loved her over the diamond. Then she saw Cullen's words on the next page.

Esther, your father was right. I found the real jewel. Your amazing, crazy da sent us on this wild hunt so we could get to know each other—the best and worst of each other. It was risky and we came close to dying, but we also were fully alive when we were together.

She stopped, held a hand to her throat. She'd thought the very same thing. But...all the deceit, all the lies. Cullen still had to prove to her that he was done with all of this.

He knew what he was doing, Esther. He was handing a true treasure over to me. But it wasn't the Levi-Lafitte Diamond. It was you, my love. I took the diamond, Esther, but I didn't sell it for profit. I took it straight to New York and gave it to its rightful owner—one of the descendants of the Levi tribe. He will display it at an official ceremony and keep it on display in the coming weeks, then donate it to a museum. The diamond is safe, Esther. I've been to the authorities and I've been cleared of any wrongdoing, due to my testimony against Charles Hogan's henchman. He is dead. His entire organization is gone, all assets frozen. It's over, finally. After I returned the diamond, I found a nearby church and I went in and rededicated my life to the Lord. And this time, I will honor it by being completely honest with you and myself from now on.

So, luv, this is me being honest. I love you. I choose you, Esther.

If you can forgive me, I'll be at the Café du Monde

*waiting for you. Even if you don't show up, I will be
waiting for you. Forever.*

Esther dropped the letters on the desk and cried. She cried
for her sweet mother, who had died giving birth to her. She
cried for her wonderful, eccentric father who'd lived his adventures through a child's eyes. He'd given her a sense of adventure and he'd taught her to take risks. He'd taken a lot of
risks, hiding that diamond, and in the end, it had cost him his
life. The people he'd trusted the most had poisoned him with
an overdose of his heart medicine. She should blame Cullen
for all of this, but her father could have confided in her and
he had chosen not to do so.

She couldn't bring him back. She couldn't bring her mother
back. And she no longer owed any debts to them regarding
this shop. She'd done her duty. The diamond was safe and
she was ready for her own adventure.

Should she include Cullen in that adventure?

Esther sat there and prayed to God to show her the way.

*What should I do, Lord? Is it time for me to move on with
the man I love, a man my father practically handpicked for
me?* A man who'd come across the world to find her.

I pick you, Esther.

Cullen's words in the letter came back to her.

What should she do?

She sat silent, waiting, listening.

And then, the last of the pendulum clocks begin striking
the hour. Six o'clock.

It was time to live her life.

With Cullen.

Cullen waited, looking at his watch, his coffee with chic-
ory growing cold. The sun was beginning to fade out behind
the spires of St. Louis Cathedral, but he didn't want to leave

yet. He'd wait awhile longer. Maybe a half hour. Maybe an hour or ten.

He'd wait forever.

And then he looked up and saw a woman with sun-streaked golden-red hair running up the street. She wore a long flowing skirt and a cute little crocheted top. She had on pretty leather sandals. And her golden eyes were shining bright, searching, searching…until she saw him.

"Esther."

He whispered the word, but now he was up and running to meet her, the traffic on Decatur, the laughter of children on the Moonwalk and the sounds of hawkers in the square all merged with the beautiful, poignant music of a lone saxophone player.

They met in front of the café.

Cullen crushed her into his arms and kissed her lips, her wet cheeks, her glorious hair, her shining eyes. "I love you."

"I love you, too. So much."

He held her there and thanked God for granting him this beautiful treasure. Then he looked down at her and smiled. "What about the shop?"

"I'm closing it down. I'd like to travel."

He laughed at that. "And where would you like to go first, luv?"

"Ireland. I want to kiss that Blarney stone."

He nuzzled her jaw. "Kiss me first."

She granted that request. And she held him tight.

While the saxophone player switched to "Diamonds Are A Girl's Best Friend" and grinned between the notes.

* * * * *

Dear Reader,

This book was a bit of a departure for me. While I love a good treasure hunt, I wasn't sure how my readers would react. So here's hoping that you've had fun going along on this adventure with Cullen and Esther.

I always love setting a story in New Orleans. It's a city of mystery and torment mixed in with spirituality and hope. New Orleans has a rich, diverse history that lends itself to a good mystery. Cullen and Esther both loved the same things, but for different reasons. And they both needed a bit of redemption. In the end, they found the real treasure and that is their love for each other and God's love for them.

I hope you'll look for my next New Orleans story. Remember Lara, the mysterious owner of the Garden District estate where Esther lives in the carriage house? Lara was out of the country during this story. But Lara Barrington Kincade returns to New Orleans hoping to find some peace and quiet. What she finds is mystery and danger and a determined photojournalist who wants to keep her safe. Look for Lara's story sometime in the near future.

Please write to me through my website, www.lenoraworth.com.

Until next time, may the angels watch over you. Always.

Lenora Worth

Questions for Discussion

1. This story is about a diamond, but the conflict is about more than just a precious jewel. Why did Esther cling to the antiques shop and the past?

2. Cullen was once a criminal, but he changed his ways. Why do you think he decided to find one last treasure to make things right? Why did he entrust the diamond to her father?

3. Esther trusted the people around her because they seemed to care. Have you ever trusted someone only to find out their friendship isn't real?

4. The theme in this story shows how chasing a false idol can bring heartache. Have you ever focused on what you thought was a treasure only to discover it didn't bring you happiness?

5. A lot of people love to collect certain valuable items. Do you think this is wise? Why or why not?

6. Antiques shops hold a lot of interesting secrets to the past. Have you ever made an important discovery while in a flea market or an antiques shop?

7. Why did Cullen come to Esther? What promise had he made to her father? Do you think he did a good job living up to that promise?

8. Why do you think Esther's assistant, Ted, gave in to greed? Do you believe Esther's father truly appreciated Ted?

9. Why did Esther's father rarely talk about her deceased mother? Do you know someone who is grieving for a loved one? Is it better to talk about this or never mention it?

10. How did Esther come to realize she needed to let go of some things? Do you think she made the right decision at the end of the book?

11. What part did the saxophone player have in this story? Do you see him as some sort of guardian for Esther?

12. In real life, evil men use others for gain. They also use money and power to stay involved in corrupt business. If you knew someone like this, would you step forward?

13. Cullen made a deal to bring down Charles Hogan. Do you think he handled this in the right way? What could he have done differently?

14. Esther cherished the stories her father told her, but she really wanted something else from him. What was that? Do you know someone who shuts down when it comes to sharing true feelings?

15. If you had a choice between an expensive diamond that could afford you everything or a happy life, which would you chose?

REQUEST YOUR FREE BOOKS!

2 FREE RIVETING INSPIRATIONAL NOVELS
PLUS 2 FREE MYSTERY GIFTS

Love Inspired®
SUSPENSE

YES! Please send me 2 FREE Love Inspired® Suspense novels and my 2 FREE mystery gifts (gifts are worth about $10). After receiving them, if I don't wish to receive any more books, I can return the shipping statement marked "cancel". If I don't cancel, I will receive 4 brand-new novels every month and be billed just $4.49 per book in the U.S. or $4.99 per book in Canada. That's a saving of at least 22% off the cover price. It's quite a bargain! Shipping and handling is just 50¢ per book in the U.S. and 75¢ per book in Canada.* I understand that accepting the 2 free books and gifts places me under no obligation to buy anything. I can always return a shipment and cancel at any time. Even if I never buy another book, the two free books and gifts are mine to keep forever.

123/323 IDN FEHR

Name	(PLEASE PRINT)	
Address		Apt. #
City	State/Prov.	Zip/Postal Code

Signature (if under 18, a parent or guardian must sign)

Mail to the **Reader Service:**
IN U.S.A.: P.O. Box 1867, Buffalo, NY 14240-1867
IN CANADA: P.O. Box 609, Fort Erie, Ontario L2A 5X3

Not valid for current subscribers to Love Inspired Suspense books.

**Are you a subscriber to Love Inspired Suspense
and want to receive the larger-print edition?
Call 1-800-873-8635 or visit www.ReaderService.com.**

* Terms and prices subject to change without notice. Prices do not include applicable taxes. Sales tax applicable in N.Y. Canadian residents will be charged applicable taxes. Offer not valid in Quebec. This offer is limited to one order per household. All orders subject to credit approval. Credit or debit balances in a customer's account(s) may be offset by any other outstanding balance owed by or to the customer. Please allow 4 to 6 weeks for delivery. Offer available while quantities last.

Your Privacy—The Reader Service is committed to protecting your privacy. Our Privacy Policy is available online at www.ReaderService.com or upon request from the Reader Service.

We make a portion of our mailing list available to reputable third parties that offer products we believe may interest you. If you prefer that we not exchange your name with third parties, or if you wish to clarify or modify your communication preferences, please visit us at www.ReaderService.com/consumerschoice or write to us at Reader Service Preference Service, P.O. Box 9062, Buffalo, NY 14269. Include your complete name and address.

LISUS11B

celebrating
15
YEARS

Love Inspired®

SUSPENSE

RIVETING INSPIRATIONAL ROMANCE

A troubled past that can't be forgotten!

THE
DEFENDERS

Someone is systematically taking everything from widow
Lindy Southerland's life. First her house, then her bank
account. She's scared her young son may be next. Former
marine Thad Pearson knows Lindy is hiding something, and
he is the only one who can protect her and her son as if
they're his own family. But keeping his scarred heart safe
proves his toughest assignment yet.

STANDING GUARD

by VALERIE HANSEN

Available September wherever books are sold.